STAY WITH THE WAGONS

A PIONEER WESTERN ADVENTURE

DAVID FITZ-GERALD

DAVID FITZ-GERALD

Cover design by White Rabbit Arts

Edited by Lindsay Fitzgerald

Welcome

Welcome back!

Ghosts Along the Oregon Trail was written as if it were a single volume rather than a series of five novels. It has been divided into five books which split the Oregon Trail into segments, or legs, of the journey. Readers will enjoy this series most when read in order, beginning with *A Grave Every Mile*.

It's great to have you back on board for the third leg of this rollicking expedition.

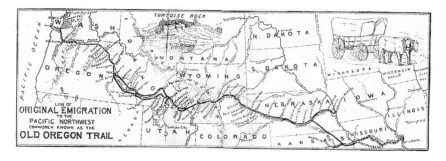

Don't forget, you can find a list of characters online at:

https://www.itsoag.com/gatot-cast.

CONTENTS

TUESDAY, JUNE 11

BENEATH THE COVER OF a quilt, I shimmy into Larkin's trousers and pull his suspenders over my chemise. Then, I wriggle into my pink floral dress. I have banished the ill-fitting corset and my mourning dress. I shall grieve no more.

After a couple of days off, our fellow travelers are eager to move on but I shall miss the scenic Red Buttes and the mighty Platte River. As the wagon wheels begin to turn, it almost feels like a new journey is beginning rather than a continuation of the one we started in Independence, Missouri.

The trail wends from our camp circle, past the discarded objects, away from the fertile river and toward the arid hills. Leaving Larkin's safe behind us weighs heavy on my mind, and I can't help feeling defeated. When Larkin died, so did his dream of being a banker, and it would be pointless to drag his strong box all the way to Oregon.

Rose cries as she walks backward and waves as if Larkin himself were standing there, forsaken. The bond between a father and his daughter is tough to sever.

Quietly, I say my own final goodbye to Larkin. Maybe I didn't love him as much as I should have, but I loved him nevertheless. If there is a Heaven and he is there, I hope that he will look proudly upon his children. I must be father and mother to them. I am strong. I *can* be both, and I shall do the best I know how to do. Whatever they need comes first.

But what about me? What do I need? Is that more important, of equal value? Or should my wants, needs, and desires be set aside? Can I love again?

Agapito's distant words echo in my memory, "Loving someone means you try to help make their dreams come true." Couldn't I do that? Couldn't I try to make someone's dreams come true? My conclusion is that falling in love is easy. Finding somebody who falls equally in love with you at the same time is impossible.

I turn back and see Cobb, bullwhip in his right hand, and baby Jenny tucked into the crook of his left arm. He nods at me, and I nod back.

Trudging along beside the wagon, I recall my promise to myself. When Larkin died, I told myself I don't need a man. I tried to expel men from my thoughts. That didn't end my yearning, but I am resolute. I can fantasize without taking action or giving in to temptation, can't I? Now, just the idea of Agapito's arms around my waist sets my heart on fire. When I attempt to blink away the image of him standing behind me in the mirror, it is merely replaced by a picture of his closed eyes as his lips gently meet my own.

The wagons move slower as we travel uphill. A quick glance over my shoulder confirms that the veritable oasis of Red Buttes looks nothing like the desert terrain stretching out ahead of us. My thoughts retreat into the past and the man I loved before Larkin. When Noah disappeared, I lost faith in love. When he returned after a long absence and married a classmate of mine, my friend Arminda, I realized that Noah never loved me. I waited years for him to return, only to discover that he never wanted to marry me. Even if I hadn't married Noah's best friend, we would never have been happy together. If he had come back and married me, instead of Arminda, perhaps I would have been happy for a while, but not forever.

The fact is, I am unlucky in love and have a history of longing for unattainable men. But what about Agapito? Am I in love with him or is he an obsession? Is he just being friendly and kind? He couldn't be in love with me, could he? How could he be? I've never met a man who fell for a woman like me. As I walk along, I wonder, could there ever be a chance for us?

I shall have to put such thoughts aside. We have a river to cross. After we cross the mighty North Platte River, which has diminished to a width of several hundred feet, we shall bid it adieu.

Even an easy crossing can be dangerous. Today we are fortunate to traverse the river without incident, but at the cost of several prime travel hours.

Beyond the Platte, the landscape transitions to rocky, dry, and arid. Nary a tree, shrub, or flower grows anywhere unless you count sage. Many emigrants complain about its smell, but I love the pungent aroma. It is hard to imagine livestock surviving on such sparse grass.

At midday, Agapito rides by on Rio. "This is Emigrant Gap. We will rest for half an hour. See the Rocky Mountains? You will spend the next week climbing them. It is different from what you are used to, no? If you see water today, do *not* let your stock drink. It is loaded with alkali, and it will poison them. If you must, give them a taste of water from your barrels."

He tilts his head slightly, looks in my direction, and smiles with his eyes. What does that look mean? A moment later, the golden horse trots toward the next wagon.

As the oxen slowly labor up the steep, sandy hill, I rejoice in the knowledge that they don't have to pull more weight than necessary. The thick sand makes walking cumbersome, and wind gusts like snow squalls force us to cover our faces with neckerchiefs again. The necessity of surviving, one step at a time, displaces romantic thoughts.

When we stop for the evening, I take shears from the provision box and cut a long slit up the middle of my pink checkered dress. Then, I climb into the wagon and don my new creation. I wonder what Captain Meadows will think as I make a similar alteration on my floral dress.

As I finish snipping, Dottie Crouse passes by and asks, "What are you doing?"

"I'm making this dress more suitable for horseback riding." I stand and demonstrate my handiwork, exposing the trousers beneath my skirts.

Dottie clucks like a chicken and says, "You shouldn't a' done that. Nope, that's not ladylike at all."

"But it is quite an improvement, is it not?"

With a huff, she wishes me a good day. Her insincere words don't trouble me any, and for some reason, I revel in her disdain.

As the sun sets, I look forward to watching the stock. We must prevent them from drinking the water in Poison Spider Creek, so three of us will stand guard tonight.

I'm proud that none of the animals drank the tainted liquid on my watch, and nobody tried to steal our stock either. The constant yips and howls of wolves keep me on my toes.

The Viper and his brothers sit beside the small crackle of a fire. A lone wolf howls in the distance, and The Viper thinks of his missing brother. How long has he been gone? Suddenly it dawns on him how quiet his younger brothers are. Usually, they are bellyaching or arguing. The Viper says, "You guys are quiet tonight."

Sloan says, "It's been a long day." He stretches out on the ground and covers his head with his hat. "I'm glad the herd is sold. Now we can get a good night's sleep."

The Radish frowns.

The Viper looks at his little brother and says, "Did you quit playing the harp?" He wouldn't admit missing the musical sound which he secretly finds comforting.

"I lost it. Can't find it anywhere. Must have dropped it."

The Viper's head slowly sways back and forth. "I swear. You can't hold on to anything, can you?"

"I'm going to miss the harp even more than my horse."

"Some outlaw you are. We're supposed to steal horses, not lose them."

"Shucks, man. I don't want to talk about that again." Despite saying he'll miss the Jew's Harp more, The Radish still grieves the loss of the red roan mare, his first horse. To change the subject, The Radish asks The Viper to tell him their plan again.

The Viper wonders at his brothers' endless need to hear the vision. After he finishes talking about plans to strike it rich over the summer, he looks at The Radish, who listens intently.

"Now tell me about the bordellos."

"It always comes back to that, doesn't it." The Viper tells his brother about how their riches will make the young man's dreams come true. The Viper tells The Radish all he can imagine to be true, but the older brother isn't any more knowledgeable about such things than the younger. "I don't know what the big deal is anyway, kid. I keep telling you, women ain't nothing but trouble. Why can't you get that through your thick skull?"

The Radish laughs and says, "I reckon I'm ready for a little bit of trouble." The Radish suggestively jostles the buckle of his gun belt, and emphasizes the word trouble. As he sags to the ground, he says, "I think about that kind of trouble all the time, and dream about it half the night."

As the evening fire dies away, The Viper wonders about his brothers. If it weren't for the promise of a life of leisure, would they stay together?

The distant wolf howls again, and The Viper thinks of his far away sibling. It was a good idea to let him go and set up a job, but The Viper didn't realize how hard their separation would be. He mashes his teeth together and leers into the darkness as if willing his brother to magically materialize. Leon is too far away, and The Viper can't stand it.

It's bad enough that Olivia is gone. As she expired, The Viper promised his sister that he would take care of their brothers. How can he take care of them if he doesn't know where they are? He must keep them together. If promising whores to the kid is what it takes, so be it. The Viper doesn't care how many pilgrims they must rob. Killing them is easy. All he does is remember Pa molesting Olivia, or Ma slapping The Radish around, and pulling the trigger becomes easy.

When they started out, The Viper felt bad. It was as if his victims were puppies, and he was no better than Ma. But then, he'd think of The Radish's scar, and convince himself, as he often told his brothers, "The world's out to get us. Hell bent on our destruction. It's you and me against the whole lot of them. We've been on the losing end long enough. Now, it's our turn." After shooting his parents, why should he care about killing strangers? Of all the people The Viper has killed, only Olivia's accidental shooting weighs heavy on his conscience.

A slight breeze tickles the corners of The Radish's handkerchief, firmly tangled into the tortured shrub. They don't know that the lost article is nearby. The Viper and his brother fail to see the missing tartan cloth.

WEDNESDAY, JUNE 12

LAST NIGHT I HARDLY slept before being roused to stand watch. At four in the morning, my tired legs carried me back to camp in time to prepare breakfast. Sleepy children gather around, as I stir mush into a froth. The boys sit cross-legged around the fire. There's a look of envy on their faces when I pass the first plate of food to Dahlia Jane.

The child takes a spoonful of breakfast into her mouth and then drops the plate, jumps back, and screams. She points at Stillman and hops up and down.

Andrew and Christopher look at each other and Rose covers her face. Stillman looks at me then back at Dahlia Jane.

I lean forward and see what has upset the girl. Then I see the creature. With my hands on Dahlia Jane's shoulders and a whisper to Stillman warning him not to move, I shush Dahlia Jane.

Instead of heeding my warning, Stillman looks down at his hand and sees the scorpion with its curled tail. A frantic, "Wah," escapes his lips as he pulls his arm away. He should have moved before yelping. The leggy spider unfurls its tail and strikes the inside of Stillman's wrist.

Stillman jumps to his feet and hops around, yipping. "I'm killed."

I ask, "Does it hurt?"

Stillman shouts over me and doesn't answer my question. "Wounded—mortally wounded!" He stomps on the crunchy spider with the thick heel of his boot. Again, he wails, "Wah. Don't that figure." He squats and picks up the flattened creature. "When I'm gone, you can bury me beside Poison Spider Creek." He moans woefully, and concludes, "I guess that's fitting."

I repeat, "Does it hurt?"

"What?"

"The sting. Does it hurt where the scorpion stung you?"

"Ah. Er. No, I guess it doesn't hurt that much."

We race to the wagon master's camp next door. Talking fast, I tell the men what happened to Stillman.

Dembi Koofai holds his hand out. Stillman holds the flattened creature between his thumb and forefinger at the end of a fully outstretched arm and drops it into the scout's open palm.

By the dim light of a tiny fire, the shy Shoshone points to the big claws, slender curled tail, and translucent, light-brown body. He tries to reassure everyone, "Almos' never bite. Tiny sting. Not ver' poisonous. Only come out at nigh'." It seems the man knows more English words than he lets on.

Dembi Koofai tries to hand the arachnid back to Stillman, but Stillman holds his hands up and shakes his head. Dembi Koofai says, "You don' like them?"

Stillman replies, "No. They look like spiders with claws. I can do without ever seeing another one of them."

Dembi Koofai's shoulders slump. "I like them. Don' know why." The reclusive scout looks down and away. Then, he retreats into the predawn darkness.

I watch Stillman's expression as his eyes follow Dembi Koofai into the darkness. I wonder whether he regrets offending the man, and something about this moment sticks in my mind.

Agapito nudges us along, telling us that the scorpions in Mexico are something to worry about but not the kind we will find along The Oregon Trail. We hurry through the rest of our morning chores so that we will be ready to march. When the sun brightens the cloudless sky, I'm glad for the early departure in hopes of a prompt arrival at our destination, wherever that may be.

The complete lack of vegetation makes the day seem even hotter. Being surrounded by rocks makes it feel like traveling through an oven. The scenery is sparse and desolate. Perhaps most people would think of this territory as ugly, but I find it beautiful in its way. For some reason, it reminds me of the mountain where the Greek Gods reside. I can imagine Zeus on a throne made of rocks perched almost anywhere along this Avenue of Rocks. I'm not sure which I find more impressive, the daunting boulders on either side of the narrow trail as we pass between them, or the view from Prospect Hill as we prepare to settle in for the night.

Stillman grabs a bucket as the children scurry about camp, tending to our daily chores. I call out to him. "Wait up. You can show me the way."

The only water source is a small hole in the ground called Willow Spring. I picture a behemoth with droopy branches, though it's hard to imagine finding such a tree along The Oregon Trail. A couple of small, twiggy shrubs grow among sparse sedges a few feet from the depression. Perhaps these are the plants that give the spring its name.

The bucket barely fits in the hole. We should be thankful to have *any* water in this arid country. I say to Stillman, "Did you ever imagine seeing a place like this?"

"No. Sure didn't." He points to the west and says, "I think those are the Wind River Mountains."

"They're stunning."

I look away from Stillman and the mountains to the west. Sometimes when I don't know how to approach a subject, I just blurt it out. I glance around to ensure we're alone and say, "What do you think of Dembi Koofai?"

Stillman looks back toward the Wind River Mountains and says, "He's very mysterious, isn't he?" Then his head jerks toward me. He whispers, "What do you mean, what do I think of him?" His body sags, and he appears deflated.

"I was just wondering." I rarely find myself at a loss for words. I start again, "I was just wondering whether maybe you and Dembi Koofai are kindred spirits."

Stillman curls his upper lip, and he repeats my words. "Kindred spirits?" He turns away and looks at the ground beyond his boots. "You mean like Carter and me?" Then he looks back up at me. "Don't you."

"I'm sorry. I suppose so. I shouldn't have brought it up."

Stillman sets the bucket down, rubs his face in his hands, and says, "That's alright. I'd rather not talk about it, but I kinda wondered the same thing. He's nothing like Carter, though. He's kind of frightening, sort of like a scorpion, I guess——scary and fascinating at the same time. Don't say anything, Dorcas. I told you, I don't want to think about anybody else."

"Never?"

Stillman frowns. "I don't know." His one-word sentences come slowly. "Maybe. Probably. Yeah. Never."

"I understand."

He says, "I gotta get back. I have watch tonight."

Thursday, June 13

After a long, dry march of more than twenty miles, we reach Saleratus Lake. Agapito warns us not to let the stock drink the smelly water. I want to pinch my nose closed. The animals must wait a little longer before we reach the Sweetwater River, but the oxen snort, and the horses dig the dirt with their hooves.

Many of us are running short of saleratus, a rising agent that is more portable and easier to use on the trail than yeast. Agapito permits a brief stop while we gather as much of the crumbly, white substance at the lake's edge as we can, and scrape the powder into small containers.

The thrilling sense of impending adventure shoots through my body, and the excitement builds within me. Our guide nudges us onward. He says, "Just a few more minutes, yes?"

I'd like to gather more saleratus, but I'm also eager to get to the most famous landmark along the trail, Independence Rock, so I hurry back to our wagon instead.

When we reach the Sweetwater River, we make camp and tend to chores as quickly as possible. The adults move as urgently as the children. Everyone races toward the enormous rock that looks like a whale stuck on a beach. I've never been to the ocean, or even seen a picture of a whale, but I have read descriptions and have a rich imagination.

Arikta outruns us all and stands beside the outcropping as we catch up. He says, "Be careful where you put your hands. Snakes like to sun themselves on the rocks." He smiles, knowing that he has our attention. "You do not want to get bitten today." I think of the scorpion that stung Stillman yesterday and decide to avoid both creatures.

The scout's warning slows our ascent. Instead of a mad scramble to the top, we scale the 125 feet of elevation more carefully than we otherwise would have.

When I reach the apex, spectators churn around me. I stand alone, a hand above my brow, in awe of the panorama.

Once I've consumed the view in every direction, I stand facing west and think about Agapito. Three days ago, the man's wandering hands encircled me. Since then, we haven't had a moment alone together, and he's barely said a word to me. It is as if he never touched me, or perhaps his impulse has passed. It isn't as if we could be together anyhow, and I plan to tell him so. I remind myself of my conviction to be a woman alone for the thousandth time.

I think of Athena, the warrior Goddess, and strike the pose of a conqueror. I feel powerful and independent with my feet separated, hands on my hips, and shoulders back. If memory serves, Athena was immune to romantic impulses. Even my wild mane of hair indulges my fantasy, blowing normally errant tresses behind me rather than into my face. Whenever a man tempts me, I will close my eyes and transport back to this immortal moment.

Christopher pokes me in the side. "What are you doing, Mama?"

The tickle of his fingers brings me back to earth. My fleeting moment as a deity is gone, but I shall savor it later. "I am trying to memorize the feeling of being here so that I will never forget it."

Christopher says, "We should carve our names in the rock. Then, people hundreds of years from now will know we were here. Maybe our names will last for thousands of years. What do you think of that, Mama?"

"Isn't it enough that *we* know? Perhaps Andrew can write about it in *The Times*. Don't you think it would be better to leave this place the way we found it?"

Christopher frowns. "But look, Mama. Lots of people have carved their names and initials here. Some have even carved the year that they were here."

"Let me ask you this, Christopher. Would you rather look at a crowded city or a wild mountain stream?"

My boy nods, understanding and seemingly agreeing. A short while later, he crouches beside the wheelwright, Schuyler Steele, tapping on a chisel with a mallet.

I've noticed that men aren't satisfied with the *feeling* of conquering milestones. They need to celebrate *themselves* with gaudy monuments to mark the occasion.

I turn away from Schuyler and Christopher as Bacon Bump reaches the top of Independence Rock with his easel and a canvas. I wave at him, chuckling to myself at the irony that his arrival further proves my theory. I shall leave the men and boys to their work.

As I walk toward Esther and Addie, I cross in front of Galusha Gains and Samuel Grosvenor. Samuel passes a dark brown bottle to Galusha, who laughs and says, "There goes the mother of that chump head."

I should walk on by, but instead, I turn and say, "Are you talking about me?"

Galusha hacks up a wad of phlegm and spits on the landmark, barely missing my feet. He laughs and says, "That girl of yours is mad as a bag full of cats in a bed of briars."

I take a step toward the man, hoping to intimidate him. "If you say one more thing about my family, I'll slap you. Imagine, grown men such as yourselves calling children names. You're nothing but a couple of worthless drunks."

Galusha says, "And you're a harlot. Not very ladylike, but somehow, it seems you got plenty of dogs sniffing around ya."

"What are you talking about?"

"Everyone says you behave like a queen bee. You got drones half your age buzzing around your *hive*."

"Buzzing around my hive?" I can't help feeling disgusted by what this vile man says and what he implies.

Galusha says, "They don't care you got a deranged kid. You got one swain caged, and still, the sorry, addlebrained curs chase you." Galusha looks me up and down. "You are a lot of woman. I'll grant you that." His sidekick laughs but doesn't say anything else.

"Not that it is any of your business, but I have taken Stillman in. He is like a son to me. Caged swain, indeed! As for sniffing dogs and buzzing bees, I don't know what you're talking about. I have taken a vow of chastity. If you ever speak to me like this again, I'll deck you, because you got one thing right, I ain't no lady."

Samuel passes Galusha the bottle again. Galusha pretends to be scared, to make it clear that he is mocking me. Samuel laughs as if entertained by his friend's comedic performance.

I lean forward with my hands on my hips. As sternly as possible, I say, "Laugh if you want to. I will not warn you again."

The belligerent men continue the charade of pretending to be afraid. I stand, not moving, trying to decide whether to slap Galusha or throw a punch at his chin. Who could blame me if I did?

As I turn away from the louts, determined to forget having encountered them today, I remind myself that I am powerful and independent. I tip my head back, spread my arms wide, and embrace the wilderness.

FRIDAY, JUNE 14

OUR EXTRA DAY AT Independence Rock isn't nearly as pleasant. In the morning, I bake as many biscuits as possible and then begin my dreaded chore, tending to the wash. I hope that Rose will help me but don't want to ask. The children work hard enough on travel days. I manage to finish scrubbing our dirty clothes when the weather turns.

A violent wind blows in from the north. It's baffling how much the temperature can plummet when the wind blows and clouds block the sun. I hang our clothes along the inside of the wagon, hoping that the gale that funnels into one end of the wagon and out the other, will not dislodge the laundry. Why didn't I bring clothes pegs with us? They would have been a useful convenience.

Standing beside the wagon with arms crossed, I look toward The Hub. Galusha leans against Andrew's post. Samuel holds his hat on his head and passes a dark brown bottle to his friend. I wonder whether they are trying to intimidate me by standing there, drinking, while facing in my direction. Galusha takes a long swig, wipes his mouth with his sleeve, and passes the bottle back to Samuel.

At Galusha's wagon, there's movement that catches my eye. His young children, Henry and Maggie, stand beside their mother, Pamela. Henry looks like he wants to run away and Maggie looks as if she'd like to hide.

Galusha's wife pulls her bonnet tightly to her head, and then watches the ground as she trots carefully from her wagon side to The Hub. She carries a small pail and clutches the ends of a shawl at her bosom to keep her wrap from blowing away.

Pamela extends her arm to hand Galusha the pail. Instead of taking what she brought him, Galusha backhands her across the face, sending her to her knees. Then, she falls back onto her behind. The pail lands on the ground, and tips onto its side. I can see that Galusha is yelling at Pamela, but the howling wind blots his words. As much as I detest watching men fight, I loathe it when a man strikes a woman. In either case, I can't stand by and watch, as others seem content to do.

Pamela cringes and scoots her behind along the dirt, sliding away from her husband. Does she hope to move faster at ground level? It is as if she thinks he'll forget she is there. Maybe in the past, she's been able to scootch away and escape a beating.

I'm halfway to The Hub when Galusha drags his wife to her feet so roughly that it looks like her arm will pop from its shoulder socket. I can feel my mouth tighten when I hear Pamela meekly whimper. If Galusha can hear the sounds his wife makes, there's no sign of it. In a loud voice, the man insults his wife. I glance at their children. Henry pulls his hat over his eyes, and Maggie drops to her knees, hiding her face with her hands.

Galusha's insults become vile. With sordid accusations that don't seem to have any basis in reality, Galusha uses explicit language to suggest that

Pamela has violated their marriage vows. I imagine the smell of Galusha's breath and the spray of his saliva on poor Pamela's face.

Samuel shakes Galusha's shoulder and points at me.

The sidekick's urgent warning isn't timely enough. Rage swells in my chest, and I barrel into the drunken bully, full force. To make sure he will not remain upright, I shove him roughly to the ground, and wrap an ankle behind one of his legs. He rolls quickly and looks up at me. Blinking fast, with his mouth hanging open, it's clear that Galusha is surprised to find himself bowled over.

I lean forward and yell at him. "You want to pick a fight with a woman? Let's see if you can handle me."

Pamela climbs to her feet and tiptoes backward, shoulders caving inward. The cowering woman covers her mouth and squeaks like a mouse, though the sound might be just my imagination. I hear her voice say, "What are you doing, Mrs. Moon?"

Galusha struggles to stand. I lift my leg, place my foot on his chest, and kick. Galusha's sidekick isn't laughing now. I turn to Galusha's friend and say, "Git." He wastes no time complying with my command and scurries away before turning to watch from a safe distance.

I turn back toward the wife-beater, and growl. "Get up. Now."

The man remains on the ground and glares at me with hatred in his eyes. I glance at the fallen pail. It looks like his wife had been baking and brought him some sweets. "What's wrong with you? Your wife brings you something to eat, and you smack her?" I lean over, right the pail, and put the treats back inside.

Galusha scowls. "Mind your own business." Then he says words that I shall not repeat, though it occurs to me to curse back at him.

I say, "Nothing would please me more. But when I see a man roughing up a woman, I make it my business. If you don't like it, get up and fight me now, you yellow-bellied coward."

He does not move.

I say, "Do we have an understanding, Mr. Gains?"

He does not answer.

A long minute passes, and I think of Galusha and Samuel pretending to be afraid of me. I didn't think it bothered me to be mocked. Now, I can't resist taking the same tone with Galusha. "Do you need help getting up?"

Galusha sneers.

"Fine then. Slither off into the grass, for all I care. If I ever catch you striking your wife, or your children for that matter, I will pulverize your face. Ya hear?"

I turn around abruptly, step forward, and run smack into Agapito. Our eyes connect for a fragment of a second. He lowers his head and nods. "Oh dear, excuse me, Agapito." As I blow past him, I think of the man I left in the dirt. Is it possible that the horrible wretch has learned his lesson? Maybe it will be good to get back on the trail. What a waste of an extra day off.

SATURDAY, JUNE 15

WE ARRIVE AT A landmark called Devil's Gate after a short, six mile trek. The name of the monument doesn't do it justice. Everyone talks about Independence Rock, but nobody mentions the splendor of this place, just a short distance, farther along. Perhaps, if it had a different name, it would be more positively regarded.

Our oxen are doing better, now that they have less to haul, but many of our fellow travelers' stock needs to graze before we can go on. Half of the crowd seems glad to rest, whereas half grumble about the miles that could have been traveled.

After we make camp the children wander off. At supper time they all return, except for Rose. We scramble to find her, but nobody knows which way she went. I wish we didn't have to let the wagon master know about Rose's latest disappearance. Boss Wheel looks perturbed, as usual, but says he saw her sitting beside a nearby grave. I thank the man and hurry off to find her.

She sits on the ground, quietly singing a lullaby. I look at the grave beside her.

A flat-faced stone, neatly lettered in crude tar, shows that Frederick Fulkerson died on July 1st, 1847. From ten feet away, the rocks covering the spot where the young man was buried don't seem enough to cover a full-grown man. He never had a chance to try and realize his dreams. The rock's arrangement makes the setting seem eerie.

Rose says, "It is so sad, Mama. He was only seventeen." She stretches her arms forward as if embracing the soil. "Poor Fred swam across the North Platte River with the stock to keep them from drifting down the river, but he caught a chill. His family did everything they could for him. His ma and pop let him ride in the wagon when he took sick, but he didn't get better. Only worse. When they arrived here, they camped for a week, hoping that he would survive and get better, but he didn't. Fred was looking forward to celebrating his eighteenth birthday in the fall, but he never recovered. That was three years ago. His ma cried for weeks, and then she died of fever too."

Rose turns away from the grave and whispers, as if she's afraid the departed soul will hear her. She confides, "Fred always wanted a girlfriend. He says his dream has finally come true. I guess he thinks that I am his girlfriend now. I don't have the heart to tell him different."

How does Rose cook up such stories? That child has a dreadfully vivid imagination. Why must she focus on such morbid notions?

Rose shakes her head slowly and her voice returns to a normal volume. She laments, "Fred misses his family, but he likes the view here."

I try to placate Rose. "I'm sure he does, dear." After a moment of silence, I mention that it is getting late and suggest that it is time to return to camp. Rose tells me that she'll be along in a while, but first she'd like to spend a little more time with Fred.

When I get back to camp, Boss Wheel grunts at me. He sounds like he's giving an order rather than offering advice or making a joke. "Put a cowbell on that urchin, why don't you?"

I grumble back at the man. "That's not very nice, and it isn't funny neither."

Boss Wheel has a coughing fit and lights a smoke. "It wasn't a joke."

There's no look of apology in the countenance of Boss Wheel. He said what he meant. It wasn't to be mean, though it surely wasn't kind. He says he wasn't trying to be funny. Does he really think that asking a teenaged girl to wear a cowbell would be appropriate? For some reason, I think to compare Boss Wheel and Galusha Gains, but it's not fair to do so. Galusha is mean spirited, but the gruff guide is honest. He likes to bark, but he does not bite. If I were him, I'd also be annoyed by Rose's frequent disappearances.

I say, "I'm sorry, Mr. Roulette. I wish we could keep Rose from wandering. We'll try to do better." Even as I'm saying the words, I know they're not true. It's impossible to watch every step that a girl her age takes.

When I return to the wagon, the painter, Bacon Bump is standing on a pyramid of boxes beside our wagon. I step back, surprised to see him there. Nearby, Christopher laughs.

How long was I gone? How is it possible that Bacon has created such a work of art so quickly? He doesn't stop to acknowledge my arrival. Instead, he continues, busily finishing the beautiful mural on the side of our wagon bonnet.

It isn't surprising to find Bacon painting, but I wonder, how does he have time for such things? Somehow, the man manages to complete his camp chores and find time for his favorite activity as well. Perhaps he asked the children, but did it occur to him to ask me whether I would mind, or whether I might prefer a different scene? Sometimes, artists are more consumed by passion for their subject matter, and less attentive to the opinions of people around them.

I tiptoe closer, hoping to avoid distracting the artist. He has masterfully depicted the furious flow of the Sweetwater River as it gushes through the rocks, and the bend of the trail through Rattlesnake Pass to the left. I tilt my head around and see his brush adding details to his depiction of a young woman beside a crude grave. With a gulp, I realize that he's painting Rose. She looks as if she's mourning the loss of the young man, Fred Fulkerson, the boy she described as if she'd known him her whole life, though they never met. How does Bacon know about that? Did he see Rose at Frederick's grave earlier?

Stepping back, I'm in awe of the beauty of the landscape painting, but the graveside scene is creepy. Perhaps our fellow travelers feel the same way when they see Rose behaving so strangely, which is far too frequent an occurrence.

With this masterpiece on our wagon bonnet, we're sure to always remember The Devil's Gate and young Frederick Fulkerson.

Sunday, June 16

In the morning, Bacon is back, working on his masterpiece. Yesterday, to me, it looked finished, but to Bacon, darkness must have stopped him sooner than he would have liked.

I wonder whether the artist will fill the canvas covering every wagon by the time we reach Oregon. I don't know why he decided to decorate our wagon now and choose this landmark, but it's a stunning landscape. We shall carry this masterpiece proudly on our bonnet, though it's not like we had a say in the matter.

Last night after Bacon said goodnight, I asked Christopher what happened. Evidently, Bacon asked for help gathering and stacking boxes but never asked permission to paint his mural.

Today, admiring Bacon's work makes me think of the rugged beauty of the Snake River forcefully carving its path through a gaping chasm. Still, I wish the landmark had a different name. Admittedly, my relationship with God is somewhat lacking. I could stand to adopt a more reverent outlook, but naming places after the Devil seems unnecessarily risky, as if we're tempting Satan to do his worst. Devil's Gate, indeed!

Our wagon bonnet is still on my mind several hours later during Sunday services. When Reverend Meadows preaches before the eye of the needle through which the thread of a river roars, I'm diligent with my amens. As he prays for our safety and our souls, my thoughts drift to poor Frederick Fulkerson's grave, just a few feet away. I clamp my eyes shut and ask God to watch over my family, even when I forget to pray, and apologize for forgetting far too often.

I don't usually laze about on Sunday afternoons. I prefer to go for a walk or ride Blizzard. Today, I relax on a blanket near the wagon and briefly visit with the children as they come and go.

When Christopher and Alvah Nye stop by to tell me that they're going off to practice shooting, I jump from the blanket when I see Honey. I'm getting more comfortable being around her, but still prefer to greet the dog from a standing position.

Christopher says, "Guess what, Mama." He doesn't wait for me to hazard a guess. He's far too enthusiastic to convey the big news. "Honey's in heat." Alvah pats Christopher's head.

My mouth becomes dry, and I begin to sweat at the thought. I imagine a pack of dogs the size of Alvah's Labrador retriever, and larger. I try to speak but find myself stuttering. Finally, I manage, "Oh." Instead of a basket full of cute little squirmy puppies, I'm picturing the hounds of Hell. The leggy creatures snarl ferociously, have red eyes, several heads, and serpentine tongues loll from gaping jaws. They paw and scratch at the ground with enormous claws, and growl frightfully. I step back and cross my arms in front of me as if my arms could protect me from their piercing incisors.

Christopher is well aware of my fears. Hastily, he reassures me. "Don't worry. Honey will be a good mother if she has puppies, and the father is friendly too."

Again, I gulp and wish that I had a tumbler of water. "The father?" I had neglected to think of him.

Cheerfully, Christopher says, "Well, there is only one other dog here, so if Honey has puppies, Landon Young's Irish setter, Chestnut, must be the sire."

I look out past Rattlesnake Pass and grip my stomach. "What about the wolves? Can a wild wolf sire a Labrador's puppies?"

Alvah grips Christopher's shoulders and tries to reassure me. "Perhaps they can, Dorcas, but Honey's not that kind of gal. Besides, we'd best not get too far ahead of ourselves here."

Not reassured, I blurt, "Good heavens, Alvah. Can you tie the dog up here when you go out on the prairie to practice? If you see any wolves, maybe you could shoot them. How about that?"

Christopher ties a rope around Honey's neck and attaches the other end to the wagon wheel. He smiles at Alvah and says, "Mama likes Honey so much, she wants to keep her nearby." I squirm when Christopher looks back at me, chuckling. Why do children delight in seizing upon their parents' weaknesses and fears? Full of optimism, Christopher says, "Maybe I can have a puppy when they come. When do you think they'll be born?"

Alvah answers, "Whoa there, partner. I said not to get too far ahead of yourself. Don't you think you're counting your chickens before they're hatched?" Alvah raises an eyebrow, looks like he's making calculations, and says, "I guess it'll be sometime in the middle of August. I reckon it takes a couple of months. I hope she doesn't have too many puppies. What if nobody else wants one?"

I look at them sternly. "Now listen, men." Christopher smiles proudly whenever I refer to him as a man. "I haven't decided yet, so don't set your expectations too high. Understand? I'm not certain about having a dog in the house."

Christopher says, "Yes, Mama," and runs off with Alvah. I'm sure he knows I'll give in. If he only knew how much I loathe the idea of having a slobbering dog nipping at my ankles, chasing my skirts, and threatening to tear into my flesh with its sharp teeth. Of course, there is more to having a dog in the house than that, but it isn't the little messes that concern me.

When the sun sets and everyone settles in, ready for a good night's sleep, I take a deep breath. It's been nice having another day off. It's been a couple of days since my run-in with Galusha Gains and his friend, Samuel Grosvenor. Thankfully, they have stayed away from me, and we survived our day, tempting fate at the unfortunately named Devil's Gate.

My eyes close and I hear a distant yip. Then, a wolf howls. Other canines answer their call. Perhaps they are all members of the same pack. Maybe rivals respond from other groups of wild dogs. They seem to be trying to outdo each other, and the howls and yelps grow nearer. I'm convinced that they know about Honey's condition. God help us.

I hope that Chestnut gets the job done quickly so that drooling wolves will prowl elsewhere.

MONDAY, JUNE 17

THE WAGON COVER RATTLES in the fierce wind. A thick frost coats the landscape and the frozen air bites my skin. The first day of summer is a couple of days away. How can the weather seem like winter this late in the year? Though we just had a day off yesterday, I don't feel like facing the trail this morning.

My stomach boils, and I hurry to the makeshift latrine. The wind threatens to dislodge a flimsy sheet that barely shields the view toward camp. I am weak and struggle to balance my weight on a rough log as I prepare to tend to my morning constitutional. My lip curls in repulsion. Having the flux is bad enough, but loose bowels in an open-air outhouse on a blustery morning is revolting, and I worry about soiling my clothing. I just did laundry yesterday.

Even after purging my innards, my stomach still roils. I think of poor Fred Fulkerson, the lad who was buried nearby and his poor mother who died a couple of weeks later. Is this how their demise commenced? It's hard not to be afraid when it seems that there's a grave every mile along The Oregon Trail.

Berta stands at the front of the line of women on the other side of the barrier, impatiently waiting for their turns. I glance at Berta on my way by, and the sour look on her face lets me know that the rancid smell hasn't evaporated in the howling wind. I'm typically blessed with regular movements. Walking away, clutching my belly, I tell myself that it can't be helped.

Stillman and the children industriously prepare for our usual pre-dawn departure, but I feel weak. Rose sneers at me as I stand with my arms crossed and watch them work. Despite feeling as I do, I'm determined to walk alongside. The starving oxen should not have to bear my weight in addition to their everyday burden.

As our team of oxen lead our wagon away from camp, I realize that I'm shrouded in a hazy fog. I don't remember my family having breakfast. Maybe they ate while I was at the privy. How long was I gone? Whatever they had, nobody provided me with a plate, not that I could stomach it anyway—just the thought of eating causes further turmoil in my gut.

The sky is still dark an hour along the rocky trail. The wind whips at my clothes and threatens to shred the fabric of my dress. Coarse sand clings to my skin and hair. There is a whistling sound within the roaring wind as the ferocious blow becomes a violent snowstorm. It's a wonder that the dry sky can find sufficient moisture to create a squall.

An hour later, we trudge through occasional drifts of several inches of snow at our feet. As much as I try not to complain, sniveling protests gather in my mind as my misery deepens. Winter's unwelcome invasion finally makes a retreat at midmorning.

I'm surprised to see Charlotte Appleyard walking with me, and I wonder how long she has been here. I don't feel like conversing, but she doesn't notice, or maybe she doesn't mind. I focus on my feet and place one in front of the other until quitting time. My tight muscles make each step a chore. Whenever a complaint threatens to tumble from my lips, I press them tightly together and force myself to continue moving forward.

When the wagons finally circle for the evening, Charlotte says that we have made twenty-two miles today. I look into the woman's face and realize that I can't remember anything she has said today, although she's walked with me almost all day.

I blink slowly as my body collapses. I can even hear the thud my body makes as it crumbles into the dirt. I feel like I'm falling through a cloud, though I'm certain that my body isn't moving. And then, darkness surrounds me.

I feel like I'm floating through a dark cave full of red cobwebs. My body feels hot. My stomach grinds. My eyes are closed, and my lids feel too heavy to open. I grumble and struggle to move. It occurs to me that I'm on my back, perhaps in the wagon, and yet I hear voices around me. Slowly, my vision comes into focus. It's like a conversation you begin to hear when you approach a crowd of people, but plainly, nobody is moving.

The sensation of a soggy rag splattering my forehead pierces my conscious thoughts. My eyes flutter, and I look up into concerned eyes. I gag, choking on my saliva. What is this man doing here?

Agapito's face moves closer to mine. I flinch when he touches me. He pinches my eyes open with his thumb and forefingers. "Maybe now you can get a good look, yes Doc?"

Another face appears above me. Hollis mutters in agreement. "Hmm. Yes. I see. The whites of her eyes are a might bit yellow."

The doctor takes my head in his hands, turns it to one side and then to the other, and tips my head back. "Her skin looks jaundiced also."

I think of my exposed chin and throat. I recall a childhood moment from long ago, holding a bright buttercup beneath Noah's chin and laughing like I didn't have a trouble in the world. Oh, how I loved that boy. Regardless of what happens later, young love stays with us, forever imprinted upon our hearts.

As Hollis returns my head to a normal position, I see the look of worry on Agapito's brow. The confident guide seems troubled today. His lower lip moves ever so slightly. If his face weren't so close to mine, I might not have seen the quiver of concern, though it is plain to see in his eyes. He turns his head slightly as he gazes into my eyes and speaks to Hollis. "It looks like fever and ague to me. We see it every year, but this looks worse than usual. What do you think, Doc?"

"That's just what I was thinking." Doc turns to his side and says, "What do you think, dear?"

I hear Charlotte's voice. "It looks like the ague to me. I don't understand it. I walked with Dorcas all day through the storm, and I didn't know she wasn't feeling well. But come to think of it, she wasn't very talkative."

Agapito asks, "What can we do for her?"

Hollis answers. "Keep her still. Try and cool her down. If she worsens, I might recommend phlebotomy. A good bloodletting will cool her core and balance her humors."

Charlotte asks, "How about a spring tonic of sulfur and molasses?"

Hollis grumbles again. "Hmm. It couldn't hurt." The doctor pensively pinches his chin between his thumb and forefinger.

Charlotte says, "How about warm milk and pepper?"

"Better for a cold than the ague, I think." Hollis steps aside and says, "But try that after the tonic, if you think it could help."

Charlotte appears at my side and wipes my hot skin with another wet cloth. Then, she looks at Agapito and says, "Good thing fever and ague isn't catchy." She pats my shoulder gently and says to Agapito, "Why don't you take care of this, and I'll be back shortly with Dorcas' treatment."

I close my eyes and hear Agapito's voice. I feel the soothing moisture against my skin and try to picture the handsome man bathing me. I hear his voice in the distance but not his words, as I tumble into a world of fantasy, a place where we are together as lovers, surrounded by bright emerald and radiant white. The dirty, dry trail is nowhere to be seen.

When my eyes flutter open again, Stillman is at my side. I clear my throat and try to speak. "I just had the strangest dream." He squeezes my right hand reassuringly, and I continue. "I don't know if we were in Heaven or here on earth, but I was married to Agapito instead of Larkin." I can feel myself struggling to speak, like saying words requires a lot of effort. "We were surrounded by green hills. You and Carter were there too. What do you make of that, Stillman?"

A hand strokes my right arm. I look down at my body and then turn to face the man beside Stillman. Agapito squeezes my hand again. I can hear myself gasp. If I'd known he was here, I wouldn't have mentioned my dream, and I definitely wouldn't have spoken to Stillman about Carter.

A few words spill from my lips. I recall saying, "I must be delirious." I slam my eyes shut and wish that I could disappear.

A hot breath in my ear precedes reassuring words. "Do not worry, *estimada*. The doctor has thinned your blood, and you should begin to feel better soon. You will be tired, but you will get better. We will take good care of you, yes? Try to rest." He pats my hand and tells Stillman that he must check on the Weavers, Carpenters, and Letts.

Evidently, I am not the only one that suffers from the fever and ague. I don't know the Weavers very well or the Carpenters either. Then I think of the German family who still grieves the loss of their patriarch and the pretty blue-eyed girl with cornsilk hair who adores Agapito. Is he on his way to Berta's bedside to hold her hand throughout the night?

TUESDAY, JUNE 18

I AWAKEN WITHIN A jostling wagon. Have the wagons started moving? Why didn't anybody bother to wake me up?

It's hot and I'm sweaty, yet I recall being cold and walking through a snowstorm. How long ago was that? My head turns slowly as I realize that Rose is talking to somebody. I turn my head in the opposite direction. There's nobody in the wagon but us.

Rose's words sound nonsensical. It's as if she speaks a foreign language. Why can't I can't understand a word she says? It is unsettling. She's way too old for baby talk. Even Dahlia Jane doesn't do that anymore. What's gotten into Rose? The strangest part is that she appears to be having a conversation. She talks a little bit, and then she's quiet. Her imaginary conversation becomes heated. Her gibberish becomes sharper, and she rapidly proceeds from perturbed to angry, and then furious. All of a sudden, she's quiet.

Her expression fades from tense to relaxed, as I watch Rose's face. She gazes down at me and exclaims, "Oh, Mama, you're awake. How are you doing?"

A wide yawn overcomes me, despite the shock of watching Rose argue with an imaginary friend in a make-believe language. I feel like stretching, but my weary body doesn't have the energy. I say, "Good morning, honey. Who were you talking to?"

Rose answers. "I don't know what you're talking about, Mama. You ain't been right since the fever overtook you."

"Oh dear, Rose. How long have I been laid up?"

"Just since yesterday, Mama."

"So what day is it now?"

Rose scowls and shakes her head. "It's Tuesday. Yesterday you fainted. Doc says you have the fever and ague. Many people are sick, but Boss Wheel says we must move anyway. At least he let us sleep in this morning." Perhaps Rose thinks the ramrod should have given us the whole day off. She spits out the phrase "insufferable tyrant."

I don't have the energy or inclination to disagree with Rose. I say, "I know, dear," then yawn, and return to slumber.

When I awaken again, I hear Andrew's voice. It sounds like he is reading aloud, and I concentrate on what he's saying. It sounds like he is reading *The Rolling Home Times*.

Andrew recites, "Beyond the Devil's Gate lies another spectacular landmark. Today, we march toward Split Rock. The view of this magnificent mountain was blocked by a blinding storm this morning. As the afternoon wore on, the rocky mountain appeared boldly against a bright blue sky as the clouds were swept away. A notch at the summit makes it look like God took a giant axe to it. Split Rock would be just another impressive mountain, if it weren't for the cleft peak. Following Devil's Gate, one wonders whether God is a lumberjack and used the same axe on both geological features. The quenching Sweetwater River flows through the first, and the crisp mountain air whistles through the crags of the second."

My son's prose moves me. "That's poetic, Andrew. What day was that?"

He drops the paper and shouts, "Mama, that was just yesterday. Today is Tuesday. Rose said you were awake earlier. It's afternoon now." He breathlessly updates me on my medical condition and the diagnosis of many others along the wagon train that also suffer from the fever and ague. "I'm supposed to give you a couple of spoonfuls of tonic when you wake up. You fell asleep so fast the last time you were awake, that Rose didn't have a chance to give you any."

The elixir tastes like chicken poop smells, or rotten eggs, yet it's also sweet, smoky, and bitter, all at the same time. It tastes more like what I would expect from poison than medicine, but I swallow the remedy without complaint.

"Did we go far today, Andrew?"

"No, Mama. Just a couple of miles. The trail isn't bad here, but so many people are sick that everyone complains about moving on." My enthusiastic son tells me that the oxen are off grazing while the travelers argue with the wagon master.

"What's the controversy?"

"It seems that somewhere ahead, one trail leads through thick sand. The other choice takes us across the river, three times in one day. The river isn't much more than a foot deep, but any river crossing can be dangerous. Boss Wheel says that the rivers will be easier on the stock. Mama, I'm worried about the oxen. They're not as bony as some of the other travelers', but I can see their ribs."

"I see." I think about our irritable leader. Though I don't often agree with the man, if he's thinking about the health of the oxen, I am with him. Addie Bull may not like all the crossings, but it sounds better to me than the deep sand route. "What do you think is the better choice?"

"We should stay by the river. The water on the other route is said to be full of alkali poisoning. So what if it might save a day of travel?"

"I think I agree with you. I'm sure that Boss Wheel knows what's best. The emigrants will not change the Boss' mind." I watch as Andrew wipes the spoon clean with a cloth and pops a cork in the medicine bottle. Then, I ask, "Did the doctor say how long it would be before I'm feeling better?"

My son frowns and looks down into his lap. "Yes. He said it could take a week or even two." He looks back up at me with worry reflected on his face. "Doctor Appleyard says that some people are never quite the same afterward. But that's mostly older people. You're not *older* yet, are ya, Mama?"

"No, son. I don't expect so." I muster as much cheer as possible while saying the words to my son. I can't remember feeling so lazy. "He's probably talking about really old people, like grandparents maybe."

"Like Reverend Hammond?"

Andrew is thinking about the kindly preacher from our hometown who died from hydrophobia last year after being bitten by an infected bat. "Yes, I think people his age have more to worry about, but remember, Reverend Hammond didn't have fever and ague."

"I know, Mama. I guess the good news is that most people don't die of it, but it is unsettling to march past so many crosses standing in the dirt along the trail. Makes me think of Pa. He didn't even live one night after he got sick. But Doc and Agapito say that Pa didn't have the same thing you got."

Though he's sitting, and I'm on my back, Andrew awkwardly hugs me. I say, "Thanks for telling me, Andrew. I'm sure that everything will be alright. You mustn't worry." When the hug is over, I ask, "Has Agapito been by a lot?"

Andrew squirms. "Yes, Mama. He spends as much time sitting with you as the rest of us do."

"Oh, I see." After a long pause, I ask, "Does that bother you, Andrew?"

"I guess not, Mama. It's just...."

I try to leave the silence and let Andrew find the words to express what's on his mind.

"It's just..." he tips his head forward as if hiding beneath the brim of his hat. "It's just that I think he's sweet on you, Mama. It don't seem right?"

"Oh, dear. It doesn't, does it?" Andrew giggles and I laugh along with him. Then I ask, "Is it because it is too soon since Pa died?"

Andrew stops laughing. "No."

"Is it because he is from Mexico?"

"No."

"Is it because he is the assistant wagon master?"

"No."

"Don't you like Agapito?"

"It's not that, Mama."

"Then why doesn't it seem right?"

"You're too old to have a beau."

I laugh. "Oh, I am, am I? Perhaps you're right, Andrew. Maybe I am too old for such silliness."

Being away from the enclave makes The Viper nervous and gnaws at his core. A few weeks earlier, he had looked forward to getting away after a long winter, but now he can't wait to get back to his home base.

After crossing the Snake River at the Three Island Crossing, like the lumbering wagons do, The Viper and his brothers make camp on the north bank. He should rouse his brothers and begin their day of travel, but instead, he lets Sloan sleep late.

The Viper steps away from camp to relieve himself and finds a nest containing four, reddish-brown, speckled eggs. He stares at the ovular orbs intently, as if boring a hole into them with his eyes, and then, one by one, he pinches each egg and laughs as the contents ooze between his fingers.

He fails to notice The Radish's Jew's Harp on the ground, a couple of feet away, at the base of yet another sagebrush.

On his way back to camp, The Viper wrings his slimy hands together, then squats and drags his fingers through the ever-present, gritty dust. His mind goes back to his first victims, not counting Ma, Pa, and Olivia.

Four men stopped by early one evening, and politely asked if they could make camp in the yard. They were on their way to St. Louis, but The Viper can't remember why. The Viper stands and gently strokes his fingers, coating them in dust. He can't remember what any of the young men looked like, or whether they were cousins, brothers, or friends.

It happened after midnight, long after the visitors had fallen asleep. The Viper's heart pounded. What if they woke up? He could have shot them, quickly, one right after the other. Before they had a chance to realize they were in danger, they'd be dead. Instead, The Viper creeped from one sleeping man to the next, placed his hand over their mouths and dragged his cold, steel blade across their necks. They died fast, and The Viper liked the gurgling sound their bodies made as they bled out.

When The Viper finished, he cleaned his blade in the dirt, and an hour later, The Viper woke his brothers, gave them five minutes to pack, and they hastily rode west on stolen horses. That was three years after The Viper killed Ma, two years after he killed Pa and Olivia. Now, eight years later, The Viper can't calculate how many innocent people he has killed. Why can't he remember what his victims looked like? Whenever he sees a dead body, he pictures the faces of Ma and Pa. It's easy to take people's belongings when he thinks of them as Ma and Pa. It isn't like he's killed innocent travelers. Instead, The Viper feels as if he's killing Ma and Pa, over and over again.

After a cup of coffee and a long, lazy smoke, The Viper presses the square tip of his boot into Sloan's side and rolls his lazy brother. "Five minutes, we ride. Drag it." The Radish is already waiting in his saddle.

WEDNESDAY, JUNE 19

WEDNESDAY IS WARMER, AND I feel a little bit better. I'm still tired after walking any distance, but at least I don't need to nap for hours after making a trip to answer nature's call. My giblets seem to have settled down, but I'm still weak, tired, and prone to fits of fever and chill.

Rattling around while the oxen pull the wagon still makes me feel guilty, but Andrew says we will only travel a few miles today. The scouts have found another good site for grazing the stock, short of the Three Crossings of the Sweetwater. I don't care how tired I am. When it's time to ford the river, I will cross on Blizzard's back rather than ride across in the wagon.

When we reach camp in the afternoon, my family builds me a throne out of boxes, kegs, and crates from the wagon. I gaze out over a lush valley, refreshing river, and rocky mountains. I'd like nothing better than to build a small cabin here and abandon the rest of the voyage. I imagine swinging an axe, chopping down trees, notching the logs, and hefting them into place. What do I know about building a cabin?

Agapito passes through on his way elsewhere. He says, "Look at you. You are the Queen of the Sweetwater, no?" I imagine looking down from the heavens at the fertile sliver separating the arid peaks. Good heavens, I've promoted myself from Queen to Goddess.

Andrew sits beside me and tells me about the Franzwa family. He has interviewed Fritz and his sons, Oskar, and Bruno. In the distance, I see the surveyor with his tripod near the bend of a river. Andrew attempts to explain how the man measures angles to determine distances and elevations. Somehow, after taking many such measurements since leaving Independence, the man has managed to make a detailed, accurate map of our journey and all its landmarks. "This afternoon, Fritz Franzwa told me about at least a dozen mistakes in the guidebook, Mama."

As Andrew finishes telling me about his interview with the surveyor, his voice cracks. I hadn't realized it before, but the boy's voice is changing. At what age is this supposed to happen? Andrew's only eleven years old. I tell myself that just because his voice is beginning to change, that doesn't make him an adult, although he has a remarkably mature intellect and professional aspirations to match.

He continues to tell me details about his interview with the mapmaker from Washington, DC, but I'm distracted. Instead of looking into his eyes or watching his face, I look at his neck and realize that his Adam's apple has become more visible, and bobs up and down as he speaks. How is it possible that I haven't noticed this change sooner? Sometimes, it's hard to notice transformations that happen before your eyes, but easy to recognize changes from afar.

Before long, I realize that I'm imagining Andrew grown and gone. It troubles me to think of my children living their own lives far away from me. It's hard not to be needed when you've taken care of them since they were born. And yet, how long has he been talking without me listening to a word he says. Suddenly, I realize that he's no longer talking about the Franzwa family. He's in the midst of listing a series of complaints about his brother, Christopher. Usually, Andrew makes a lot of sense, but I can't understand why he would call his brother lazy.

When Andrew pauses, I say, "Christopher's only nine years old. It may not sound like a big difference between you and him, but two years is a long time for boys your age. I don't know of a harder working nine-year-old, Andrew."

"Oh, Mama. You're always taking his side. Sure, he works hard, but not for us. Just for Alvah." The pitch in Andrew's voice rises as he protests. I suspect that Andrew would like Christopher to do all of the work in camp so that Andrew can spend all of his time chronicling our journey.

As if summoned, Christopher runs into camp and skids to a stop in front of me. Andrew frowns at Christopher. "Where you been?"

Christopher says, "At Alvah's."

Andrew catches my eyes, and the look on his face says, *See, I told you so.*

Christopher blurts, "Chestnut was there, and..." he looks around and blushes. He tries to speak again. "Honey was there, and..." The distress on his face shows that he can't find words that children are allowed to say to describe what happened. He stumbles into a solution, "Well, let's just say they got married, and soon we'll have puppies." He seems delighted to have found a way through his verbal dilemma. Enthusiastically, he chirps, "How about that!"

I try to match his enthusiasm, though I'm not sure I'm hoping for the same outcome he is. I warn him, "You can never be sure about such things, Christopher."

The boy argues. "Yeah, but I saw it. I saw it happen. So, I'm sure there's going to be puppies, Mama."

At Christopher's age, it's hard to face the reality when what seemed like a sure thing doesn't pan out. I try to warn him. "I understand what you're saying, Christopher, but just because you saw it doesn't mean it took. Sometimes it does, and sometimes it doesn't. You can't be sure until later."

Christopher sits beside me and Andrew wanders away. It's like they had a bargain that they would take turns sitting with me while I'm ill. He's quiet for a while, and I can see the uncertainty on his face. I can always count on Christopher's lips to give away his thoughts. Somehow, he bunches them together and shifts them up and down when he's not sure about something. As I'm watching his face, I realize his features are more chiseled than I remember them being. His round, boyish face is changing. I sigh, and think about Andrew's maturing voice. Christopher looks over at me and says, "Why are you staring at me, Mama?"

I tell him, "Because you're so handsome."

His eyes roll and he makes a gesture beside his cheek to let me know he thinks I'm crazy. Then he sits closer and talks about all of the horses that travel with us. It's a subject we both enjoy, and time floats by like clouds in the sky.

After a while, Rose relieves Christopher. I watch as he races across the circle of wagons, back to Alvah Nye's camp. I'm aware of Dahlia Jane playing with Bess and Joe beneath Cobb's wagon, next door.

Rose sits beside me for a while. Sometimes, she sits with her pencil touching her cheek, as if she doesn't know what to write in her journal. Today, the words seem to flow like the current of the Sweetwater River. Despite the sound of flowing water nearby, and the voices of my fellow travelers, I can hear the urgency of the pencil lead scraping the pages in Rose's diary. I wonder whether her written words would be easier to understand than the words she speaks out loud. She doesn't seem like she wants to talk to me now, but I am content to sit quietly with her beside me.

As the day comes to an end, and I watch the sun set, I think about the changes in my family. My three oldest children are so young yet, but it's hard to deny seeing the signs of who they will be as adults. It's hard not to worry, but most of my concerns tend to revolve around Rose.

Thursday, June 20

How hard can it be to sit on a horse all day long? Normally, it wouldn't faze me. I never realized how much work the simple act of sitting up straight and bearing my own weight required. Perhaps a better way to convalesce is to remain supine, sheltered by a wagon bonnet, and covered with a thick quilt. My sickness has caused me to miss enough of the journey already.

Blizzard splashes across the shallow river. We walk to a slight prominence near the bank, turn to face the procession of wagons, and watch the slow-moving train make its way across the water. A short distance away, Boss Wheel sits on Clipper. He removes a spyglass from his pocket, pulls the telescoping cylinders forward, and gazes out over the horizon. When satisfied with his reconnaissance, he digs a pipe from his pocket and monitors the emigrants as he sends tendrils of smoke skyward.

Today, I feel like Boss Wheel, sitting on my horse's back and observing people. The comparison makes me chuckle. It's hard to picture myself smoking a pipe. A spyglass, however, would be useful.

Agapito guides travelers as they enter the river, and Arikta greets them as they roll up the bank after fording. Dembi Koofai must be scouting ahead or hunting. Andrew says that we are nearing the lands inhabited by Dembi Koofai's people.

Andrew leads the wagon master's wagon across the river. I watch as Stillman walks along one side of our wagon while Christopher splashes along on the side nearer to me.

My mind wanders. Christopher has experienced a growth spurt. The scrawny lad has grown stronger but hasn't complained about his tight trousers. It can't be easy getting dressed every day. How many inches can a boy grow in two months? Christopher notices me watching him. He tips his head toward me and touches the brim of his hat, just like Alvah does. Christopher needs clothes that fit him properly. When he passes me, he tells me that I'm looking better.

The second river crossing goes as smoothly as the first one did. Even so, three river crossings make for a long day.

At the third crossing of the Stillwater River, as Andrew fords with Boss Wheel's team, he has a pained expression on his face and grabs his stomach.

Worry floods through me. Is Andrew coming down with fever and ague? I remember him telling me that he gets a stomach ache when something bad is about to happen. I glance at the wagons that have yet to cross and consider riding forward to warn Agapito, but what would the man think? Andrew's predictions are never wrong. It is only their lack of specificity that makes them hard to act upon. Indecision vexes me.

Stillman and Christopher guide our oxen into the river. I've almost talked myself out of my concern when Hardtack, the lead ox on Stillman's side accelerates. Scrapple, the ox on Christopher's side falters.

My body tenses as Christopher races toward the stumbling ox. When he whacks the bullock on its hindquarters, I grimace. Then, Christopher falls. It is as if whatever caused the beast to stumble has also tripped up Christopher.

I scream as the boy falls beneath the ox and disappears beneath the water's surface. My legs press into Blizzard. We rush toward the place in the river where Christopher had been, as the oxen climb the riverbank.

Panic overwhelms me at the sight of Christopher's body, cradled in Stillman's arms. During my hasty dismount, I forget about my sickness and weak condition. My legs fail to support me, and my body crashes into the water. I remember being clumsy as a teenager and, if I must be honest, well into adulthood. In addition to being a good rider, my skills include swimming, but for some reason, I don't seem capable of finding the surface of the water in the shallow river. I gulp for air, but swallow water instead, and darkness claims me.

Perhaps a minute later, water spurts from my lungs, and my eyes blink open.

Agapito kneels beside me. "What happened?" My gaze shifts toward my bosom. Why is he touching me there?

"You were trying to drown, *estimada*. I could not let that happen."

Christopher laughs, and I turn toward the sound. Of course Agapito and Christopher know that I wasn't trying to drown. People often joke around after surviving dangerous situations.

Christopher lies on the hillside next to me. A sense of relief washes over me, and I try to sit up. I've never had difficulty doing so before, but don't have the strength to sit up or climb to my feet. I'm grateful when Agapito extends his hands and helps me stand.

"Oh, Christopher. You are alright. I was so worried."

"Of course I'm alright, Mama. I'm not the one who tried to drown." He attempts to stand, and I can see the pain on his face. Agapito says, "Maybe you should wait for the doctor, no?"

Stillman says, "I think Christopher's arm is broken."

Agapito sends Stillman to get dry clothes and blankets for Christopher as Hollis and Charlotte step forward. Hollis pats my shoulder and tells me to let him take care of Christopher, and Charlotte will look after me.

Charlotte places a hand on my forehead and sternly orders me to bed. "What are you thinking? Don't you know how serious an illness the ague is? You shouldn't be out of bed for days yet, let alone riding all day, and then going for a swim."

I think of Charlotte's loss and the death of her son, Martin. It seems like ages ago now, but it's only been a month. Christopher could have died this afternoon. I don't know the extent of his injuries, but we should consider ourselves lucky. Then, I remember seeing Andrew grabbing his stomach. "Yes, Charlotte, I should have known better." Worry niggles in my core.

"Could you check Andrew and make sure he doesn't have the ague also? He clutched his stomach earlier. Maybe he is sick."

"Don't worry yourself now. Hollis and I will look after your boys, and when we've got them patched up, we'll send them to you."

Christopher's tight-fitting trousers cross my mind and I recall Charlotte's dolls. "I've got another favor to ask, if you don't mind, dear." As if Charlotte doesn't have enough to worry about.

"Of course, don't be silly. How can I help?"

Charlotte says, "Christopher strikes me as a rugged sort of boy, isn't he?"

I nod weakly.

Charlotte continues. "Well, I was working on some buckskin trousers because we were told to have lots of presents ready to give to the Indians. I think I've got a set that are just his size. Do you think he would like them?"

I assure her that he would, and thank her with all the enthusiasm I can muster.

"Don't mention it, dear. It's as good as done." Charlotte tucks a blanket beneath my chin, and I'm transported through time to when my mother used to say goodnight to me as a girl. In my head, I tell Charlotte what a good friend she is. My eyelids sag closed and I feel myself falling asleep.

After who knows how long, I awaken, surrounded by my children, and Stillman holds Dahlia Jane in his arms. It's rare for them all to be in the wagon at once, and my heart races. Is there something wrong with me? Am I at death's doorstep? I take a fast inventory of my senses and decide that I'm alright. Not my usual self, but surely that's not why they've gathered around me. Then, I notice Christopher, outfitted in buckskin and fringe from head to toe. I flashback to my childhood and think of Noah, who yearned to be a mountain man. I try to blink away the memory, and to my son, I say, "You look very handsome, Christopher. Are you off to trap beaver?"

Christopher laughs and says, "Not yet, but soon, Mama." Doesn't he know that times have changed? There are far too few beavers remaining in the mountains, and their market value has declined. He points at the sling over his shoulder. "Maybe after my arm heals." I'm not sure whether he's prouder of the new clothes or his arm in a splint.

Stillman says, "Christopher didn't flinch when Dr. Appleyard set his arm." Christopher stands taller, and his chest puffs out as Stillman praises him. "He didn't make a sound. If it were me, I'm sure I would have screamed out in pain."

"I'm just glad you're alright, Christopher." I glance at Dahlia Jane, Rose, and Stillman, then at Andrew. I'm glad everyone is doing so well, especially since their mother can't do a thing right now."

There's a frown on Rose's face, but as he often does, Andrew speaks for the children. "Don't worry, Mama. We'll take care of everything, you'll see."

"I'm sure you will, Andrew. Are you alright? You're not coming down with something, are you? You were grabbing your stomach when we crossed the river."

"No." Andrew glances at Christopher, then back at me. He snaps, "I'm fine. Maybe I was just hungry."

It is always apparent to me when Andrew isn't being truthful. If it weren't for the presence of others, he might admit that he had a premonition. "You look hungry, Andrew. Christopher is too big for his britches, and meanwhile, Andrew, that shirt is way too big for you now."

Andrew laughs and says, "Just like you, Mama. We're wasting away. Maybe it's because you quit baking cakes and pies."

Dahlia Jane pouts. "You promised to bake us a cake, Mama."

"You're right. I did, and I forgot all about it. When I'm feeling better, that's the first thing I'm going to do. How does that sound?" Dahlia Jane smiles and nods, and I realize that she isn't the only one. All of the children, and Stillman, too, seem to agree with her.

Dahlia Jane says, "You'd better not forget again, Mama." There's nothing like a broken promise to a child to make one feel guilty.

FRIDAY, JUNE 21

Today is the first day of summer. A few days ago, we traveled through a ferocious snowstorm, but Andrew says there is no chance of bad weather today.

I feel like a bird in a cage. The children barely let me step a foot off the wagon. I long to ride out on the prairie or walk along the wagon train and talk with friends, but haven't the energy to do so. My jailers don't need to be so vigilant, for I am like the bird sitting in a cage with an open door.

Instead of sleeping all day, as I did a couple of days ago, I don't seem to be able to stay asleep very long. The fever comes and goes. The relentless sun illuminates the wagon cover above, and sweat drenches my body. Then, despite the heat of summer, a chill overtakes me. I pull a thick blanket over me, and shiver. A few minutes later, I'm sweating again and push the quilt away. I yawn nonstop, but after napping for a couple of minutes, I twist and turn, trying to find comfort on the stiff boards that serve as my mattress.

The long day should be over already, but we haven't even stopped for our midday break. I could sew, but would rather spend the day counting my fingers. I could read, but don't seem to be able to get comfortable enough to concentrate on the words as they pass my eyes. Truth be told, I'm not in the mood to do anything but stew like a tomato in a pot.

Finally, the wagon comes to a stop. I hear voices in the distance, but there isn't anybody nearby. It is like everyone abandoned their wagons. The docile beasts have learned to rest whenever they have a chance.

The hot air is still, and I'm having a feverish moment. Why haven't the children checked on me? Could they have forgotten that I am alone in the wagon? I think of all the times I rode off on Blizzard or wandered down the line of wagons. Perhaps they've grown so used to my long absences that they don't think of me when I'm out of sight. They are getting older and more independent, and instead of looking to me when they need something, they look to each other, or somebody else. Stillman is a big help, and Christopher spends as much time with Alvah as he can. And the guides in the next wagon seem as fond of the children as the children are of them, except for Boss Wheel, of course. I admonish myself for thinking pitiful thoughts. My children need me, even if they believe they don't.

I talk myself into venturing from the wagon. While the train has stopped, it is an opportune moment to tempt a snake. My lips and cheeks stretch wide into a cavernous yawn, and I groan as my legs search for solid footing beneath me. A second yawn quickly follows the first as I scoot my backside along the planks toward the wagon's rear. Simply sitting up makes me dizzy, but I inch toward the exit nevertheless. I steady myself with my hands on the back of the wagon while lowering myself toward the ground. I've done this a thousand times before, but now, for some reason, my feet don't find solid ground. My shoulder hits the ground with a squishy thump.

Why have we stopped in a swamp? I groan as moisture penetrates my clothing and wets my skin.

"Mama, what are you doing?" I labor to sit up as Andrew runs toward me. "I was just coming to get you. We've reached Ice Springs, Mama. I wish you could see it. Agapito showed us how to dig through the soggy peat. Beneath the dirt, a couple of inches down, a river runs underground, and beneath that, there are sheets of ice. It's the purest ice you ever saw. And guess what, Mama? Mrs. Appleyard has a bucket with a crank on the top. Inside the bucket, there's a pewter canister. She packed salt and ice around it and handed the bucket to Dr. Appleyard. She says that her husband is spinning sugar and cream together. Oh, Mama. Can I help you get up off the ground?"

Andrew helps me stand, and I shiver as he explains the science of freezing cream into a sweet treat. Then, I remember Mr. Ray in Independence telling me about this place. I know he just wanted to sell some of his prime peppermint extract. I direct Andrew to where he can find the distillation, and look for a concealed place to answer nature's call.

I tell Andrew to hurry and bring the peppermint flavoring to Charlotte. With everyone distracted at Ice Springs, I manage to take care of my business behind our wagon without collapsing. If anyone is watching, I can't help having exposed myself. It isn't decent, but I haven't the energy to walk far enough away to avoid being seen. As it is, I can barely lower and raise myself without falling to the ground. Just a couple of days of the ague have turned me into an invalid. What if I never get my strength back? I remember Hollis saying that some people are never the same again.

Off in the distance, everyone cheers. The jubilant voices make me think of a Fourth of July celebration. I yearn to join them as another yawn stretches across my face. I extend my arms and drag my body up into the wagon. After drawing the bonnet closed, I struggle to remove my dress. The simple act of changing my clothes makes me feel like I have run for miles without stopping for a break. I stretch my body across my wooden mattress and feel beads of sweat on my forehead.

How long have I slept? Someone shakes my shoulder. I'm feeling groggy, open my eyes slowly, and see Agapito. My heart thumps, and I feel feverish again. Agapito helps me sit forward, propping something soft behind me. "I have a treat for you, *estimada.*" He dips a tin spoon into a bowl. "Close your eyes and open your mouth, Dorcas." I remember the first time he said my name and how exotic it sounded when he said it. I feel vulnerable, waiting for what comes next.

I open my eyes and close my lips as Agapito pulls the spoon from my mouth. The smooth, sweet cream coats my tongue. A vibrant, minty flavor dances on my taste buds and makes me feel like my old self. The frosty dessert melts in my mouth and cools my fever. My eyes find the corner of Agapito's mouth, and my heart melts at the sight of a slight smile elevating the dimples on the man's smooth cheeks. In a quiet voice, he says, "*Te gusta?* You like?"

My eyes should look away from his face. Looking directly at him for this long feels far too intimate. He looks away from me briefly to scoop another spoonful of ice cream into my mouth. He looks back at me with each bite, and I can't help thinking that his eyes shine. Often, they are melancholy, but not today.

Without looking away from him, I remind myself of all the reasons that we can't be together, but at this moment, those excuses don't sound very convincing. Perhaps reason will prevail once he walks away, but I'd be powerless to refuse him if he courted me right now.

It's been almost two weeks since Agapito wrapped his arms around me in front of a mirror. I remember him telling me that he was sad and lonely, but he looks neither sad nor lonely now. It is as if, briefly, he has forgotten his promise to Merced, and I have been cured of fever and ague. I neither feel too hot nor chilled and don't wish to be somewhere else.

I could look at Agapito's face for hours without growing tired of doing so. There is no need for words. If only this moment could last forever, but far too soon, the tin spoon scrapes the bottom of the bowl, and distant voices draw near.

A tear forms in the corner of my eye as my children climb aboard, and Agapito looks away from me. The guide tells them, "Do not stay long. It will be time to roll again in a few minutes." He smiles at me and awkwardly makes his way past the children in the crowded wagon.

After listening to exuberant chatter about crushed ice, chilled lemonade, and frozen desserts, I ask about Christopher's injuries. The boy smiles proudly as his brother speaks for him. "You wouldn't believe it to look at him. His arms and legs are covered in scrapes and bruises. There's an ugly black and blue mark on his hip. He got beat up pretty good, but he never complains. And the oxen don't seem to know he has a useless arm."

With nine sharp blasts, the children pile off the back of the wagon. Some moments, brief as they are, make one wish that they could capture them and relive them repeatedly. If only they weren't so fleeting.

Andrew is the last to leave. He says, "See you at suppertime, Mama."

Saturday, June 22

The second day of summer is sweltering hot. The broiling sun, dusty road, and crippling heat create such misery that even our leader has had enough. Boss Wheel calls a halt after only a few hours of travel. After seven miles, the oxen are weary, and Dembi Koofai has found a grassy meadow for them to graze.

I have enough energy to launder the dress that I wore during my fall from the wagon at Ice Spring. Then, I while away the day by the riverbank, dipping my feet into the flowing currents of the Sweetwater, admiring the distant haze of the Wind River Mountains, and relaxing around camp as the children attend to their chores.

No matter how hot it gets, the young lovers, Violet Appleyard and Pious Bull, Junior, always have sufficient energy to traipse around the circled wagons, literally walking circles around the rest of us. By the time our wagon train reaches Oregon, Violet and PBJ will probably have logged enough miles to have walked there and back again. They never tire of spending time together, and rarely seem to interact with anybody else. If there were an evening when they didn't stroll the perimeter of our gathered wagons, there might be cause for alarm.

When Charlotte stops by to check on me, she sits beside me in the meager shade beside the wagon. As Violet and PBJ pass us, Violet waves with her right hand and says, "Hi Mother," to Charlotte. PBJ tips his hat with his left hand. Between them, their joined hands swing, carefree, and soon they've passed us by, once again.

I try to imagine what Charlotte looked like, when she was Violet's age. I inquire, "Does Violet favor you, dear?"

The homesick woman wistfully sighs. "It's like looking into a magic mirror. Sometimes, it reminds me of when Hollis and I were courting when I see them together, but we never spent as much time together as they do. They're practically married already."

"They seem to be a perfect match. Have they ever had a disagreement?"

"I can't remember seeing them quarrel, and Violet has never complained about PBJ, at least not to me, she hasn't." Charlotte is quiet for a moment, and I glance her way, wondering what she's thinking about. She places a hand on my forearm and says, "Do you mind if we talk about Martin?"

"Not at all, dear," I say, hoping to offer solace.

She tucks her chin to her chest, and closes her eyes for a moment. "I think of him all the time. Sometimes I talk to him like he's still alive, and sometimes I point to things as if he could see them, just as I do." She turns her head toward me and places her hand on her chest. "Hollis and Violet seem afraid to mention Martin's name or talk about him. I wish they'd talk about him more often. I'll never get over losing him. It pains me that he went so young. I can't stand the thought of banishing him from my mind." Charlotte smiles and waves as Violet and PBJ complete another lap. "The fact is, I'm never happier than during those moments when I'm thinking about Martin." She sniffles. "He may be gone, but when I think about him, it's like he's still with me. I can't stop loving him just because he's gone. And why should I?" Charlotte looks away, pauses for a moment, and then turns quickly back to face me. "Oh, Dorcas, just listen to me carrying on. I declare!"

Sympathetically, I say, "Thanks for telling me. I will try to remember."

Charlotte confirms that it will make her happy whenever I mention her son in the future. I think of the ordinary looking young man with brown hair and green eyes. All he wanted was to catch young Cassie Meadows' eye. I wish I could recall more about him so that I could bring him up more frequently.

Then, Charlotte says, "When Violet gets married, she cannot move away."

I ask if there's been talk of marriage between Violet and PBJ.

Charlotte confirms that she has overheard them talking about the future, but so far PBJ hasn't asked Hollis for his daughter's hand. She goes on to say, "Of course, we already love PBJ. Hollis had better give them his blessing. I don't care if they have a fancy wedding, but when they're married, assuming they get married, we have to follow them wherever they go. Martin is gone, I've lost my home in Virginia, I can't lose Violet too. That's all there is to it. I don't care if I have to follow them all the way to the moon. Wherever they go, I go. Hollis had better not have other ideas."

It's hard to think of a time when Hollis and Charlotte have seemed out of sorts with one another. I can't imagine Hollis having other ideas, but moving to Oregon was Hollis' idea.

I yawn and ask Charlotte if she'd like a drink of water, or perhaps some lemon-flavored water. She jumps to her feet and insists that I allow her to fetch it. I'd like to protest, but another yawn betrays my weariness. Tomorrow, it will be a week since I first began suffering from the ague. I expect to make a full recovery, and it can't happen soon enough to please me. When Charlotte returns with tumblers full of sweet and sour refreshments, I chuckle as the young lovers stroll by again.

Charlotte lifts an eyebrow and asks what's so funny.

As she sits back down beside me, I tell her that I was imagining my boys, Andrew and Christopher, strolling with their favorite gals. I add, "But that won't happen for ages."

Charlotte says, "Don't be so sure. The years sail by, and before you know it, your little darlings become adults. It's sad when they don't need you anymore, but what can you do?"

Stillman steps into camp with a bucket of water, and I groan. "Oh, Charlotte, it's my turn to stand watch tonight."

Stillman interrupts our conversation. "Oh no you don't, Dorcas. It's too soon. I'll take your turn tonight."

Sunday, June 23

Sunday is just like Saturday, except that all the chores are done, and the children have enjoyed spending most of the day off. Andrew sits beside me and looks at me with a worried look. He says, "We're going to miss the Sweetwater River." The simple statement seems ominous. I've come to understand that something terrible lies ahead when he says things like this. What next? After all the terrible things that have happened already, it doesn't seem like we should have to contend with any more hardship. Whatever is coming, we'll have to face it. I'd rather not hear about it now.

Hoping to sidestep Andrew's concern, I agree with his prediction. "After the muddy rivers we've followed, the clear, cool water has been most refreshing. I think it's the best tasting water we've encountered."

In an ominous tone, Andrew warns, "It won't be long now until we reach the Snake River."

I feel a chill wash over me and shudder. "I don't feel so good, Andrew."

He suggests that I take a nap and reminds me that I've been sick. After an hour's rest, alone in the wagon, sleep doesn't come and I decide to give up and go visiting instead.

How long has it been since I paid my friends from home a call? It's been at least five days. Since being afflicted with the ague, I've hardly conversed with anybody, aside from the doctor and his wife. Though the urge to laze about remains strong, the thought of seeing neighbors perks me up a tad. It doesn't need to be a lengthy visit, and I can easily return to the wagon should fatigue overtake me.

After a brief but pleasant visit with Cobb, I venture into Bacon and Esther's camp, but Esther and baby Plumjohn are alone. "Good afternoon, Esther. Where's Bacon today?" I inquire.

Esther rises, shrugs, and turns away from me, saying, "How should I know?" She sets the baby down, picks up a broom, and begins to sweep the side of the wagon, a chore that has never occurred to me.

I say, "Is everything alright, dear?"

Without turning from her task, in a matter-of-fact tone of voice, she says, "Everything's fine."

The straw fibers of the broom scratch noisily against the woodwork, and many seconds go by. Finally, I offer, "I'm glad to hear it." Certainly, Esther must know that I've been sick, but she doesn't seem curious to ask how I'm doing or offer any sort of polite pleasantries. Another several seconds pass by. It takes some effort to sincerely say, "Have a pleasant afternoon, Esther."

Esther stops sweeping for a moment, then returns to her work. Though I never said a word about Bartholomieux to Rose or anybody else, I may have to accept that Esther will never forgive me for revealing her secret. A few short steps later, I find the Bull family relaxing in their camp, sitting cross-legged on a large blanket as if enjoying a picnic. Pious and Addie sit side by side. Charlotte's daughter, Violet, sits beside Addie, and PBJ relaxes beside Violet. The lovebirds remain inseparable. PBJ's sister, Mary, sits between her older brother and her younger brother, Leander.

Addie climbs to her feet, clucking. "Are you supposed to be up and around? Let's find you somewhere to sit down. Can we do that, Pious?"

I protest, "Good heavens, no, dear. I need to stretch my muscles and move about a little. I've been cooped up far too long." I turn my head and yawn, hoping that Addie didn't see the evidence of weariness. A splash of color on the side of their wagon bonnet catches my eye. How did I miss seeing that on my way by? I gasp and say, "Oh, Addie. I had no idea you were sporting such a... a..." I want to say masterpiece, but I'm not sure that's the best word to describe what I see. "When did Bacon paint that?"

The mural on the side of the Pious family's wagon features Leander opening Larkin's safe, beside the chocolate-colored North Platte River, with the striated Red Buttes in the background. Addie tells me that Bacon painted the scene a couple of days ago. Perhaps it's the angle of the sun that makes the fresh paint look like it's still wet. After a moment, I realize that my thoughts have run away from me. That wasn't just the day we parted with Larkin's precious strongbox. It was also the day that I stood before a mirror and was surprised by Agapito's unexpected embrace.

A voice interrupts my reverie. "Mrs. Moon," Leander says.

I turn toward the family, still seated on the blanket.

Addie's son says, "Why don't we go down to the river? How about that? Ain't no reason to hang around here any longer."

Pious corrects Leander, emphasizing the first two words in the sentence. "There is no reason to hang around here any longer." He closes the book that he had been reading, uncrosses his legs, and stands. "I suppose we've studied the Bible enough for today." The family follows Pious' lead, and he adds, "A brief stroll would be welcome."

Addie looks nervously at Leander, and back at Pious. She seems to want to say something, but refrains from speaking. Is her fear of drowning on her mind, or does something else trouble her?

PBJ folds the blanket, tucks it under his arm, and his fingers weave between Violet's as if their palms were naturally drawn together by magnetic force. They follow Pious, and Leander is directly behind them.

Addie says to Mary, "Come along, dear."

Mary sighs, and says, "Oh, alright."

Addie looks over her shoulder, across the ring of wagons and whispers. "Mary was hoping that a young man would come calling on her this afternoon."

I offer, "Oh, I understand," but no details are forthcoming and I wonder which young man has caught Mary Bull's fancy.

Leander darts back toward us and he says, "Don't worry, Mrs. Moon. We're almost there."

My fingers reach for my hair, and I realize that I'm poking at strays. Why does the boy think I look worried? Do I look sicker than I feel? "Thank you, Leander."

He says, "It's too bad, isn't it."

The boy is quiet for a minute, and finally, I agree. "It sure is."

He shakes his head slowly, and frowns. "That was such a fine safe to have to leave behind like that. What a pity."

"I know," I say with a sigh. "It sure is." I thought he was going to say that it was too bad that I had the ague, but I should have known the young man who wants to be a banker, just like Larkin did, was still thinking about the safe.

I'm sorry it's gone, but I regret hauling it as far as we did. We should have abandoned it sooner.

Monday, June 24

After Reveille, Arikta passes through camp. "Make sure your kegs are full. Water the stock good. We are leaving the Sweetwater River for the day."

The morning is cool. I still have moments of fever followed by a chill, however, they aren't as frequent and don't last as long. I'm glad that after a week of suffering, I feel stronger.

Hollis warned against exerting myself too strenuously. I walk along the rocky trail for an hour as the oxen pull the wagons uphill. Then, I retreat beneath the wagon cover as the blazing sun warms the day, even though the oxen must bear my weight. As the wheels roll up a rock on one side, they fall from a rock on the other. The wagon bounces and jostles, pitching my body about as I hold onto the boards that serve as my mattress. The rough trail rattles my bones and makes my teeth clatter. Though it might sound dramatic to say so, it is a fact that I can attest to. Ague or not, there's no rest and relaxation to be had within the wagon today.

I climb carefully from the back of the wagon and ask Stillman to saddle Blizzard. My horse's easy-flowing gates make me think of a padded rocking chair on the porch. I shall spend the day in the saddle beneath my wide-brimmed hat rather than being pitched about the wagon.

I'm glad that the oxen had a good rest on Saturday and Sunday because the steep, rocky trail must seem like torture today. I look toward the Heavens and say a prayer for them. Thank goodness I finally had the sense to let go of Larkin's safe and my heavy woodstove.

Near the top of Rocky Ridge, the wagon careens wildly from a particularly violent upheaval of stone. After we crest the summit and begin our descent, an ear-splitting scream pierces the air. One screech desperately follows another.

The clatter of horse's hooves precedes Agapito's arrival on Rio from the front of the train as Arikta trots forward from the back on Howl. I turn Blizzard toward the sound and see Addie on her knees, pounding a flat boulder with her fists. Pious kneels beside her, trying to calm his wife. PBJ hugs his sister, Mary. What happened? Where's Leander?

I can't figure out what's wrong with Addie until I see the limp body of Leander a dozen feet away. His body is practically sliced in half, and it's plain to see that the wagon wheels rolled across his midsection. I wish I hadn't looked at him. I wish I could console my friend, but I don't feel strong enough. Instead, I cover my face and feel hot tears on my fingers. The urge to vomit is strong.

I take my hands from my face and look down the hill at the steep incline. Even through blurred vision and tears, the trail appears rough and dangerous. Arikta leads the Bull family's oxen over the top of the ridge and down the other side.

Once again, Agapito is left to deal with a grieving family during the worst moments of their lives. Bobby and Serena, in the next wagon, agree to let Leander's body ride in the back of their wagon. The assistant wagon master gently coaxes Addie to her feet. Pious follows on wobbly legs. The lost look on the man's face shows a man whose deep faith is suddenly shaken. He blindly follows Addie and Agapito as if he doesn't know what else to do. PBJ and Mary cling to each other, just behind their father, and Violet follows PBJ with her head hanging low.

The remaining wagons roll across the same trail and are tossed by the same rock that claimed the poor boy's life. I've known Leander since he was born. Recently, when our oxen trampled over Christopher and he almost drowned, I was forced to imagine my child's death, yet now, I can only imagine what my friends are going through. Losing Larkin was bad enough. I feel my body curling inward at the thought.

When the last wagon in our train has crested Rocky Ridge, I remain frozen at the spot where Leander died. The dry wind swirls about, and I gaze off into the distance. I haven't the slightest desire to move from this spot. It is as if the boy's spirit remains here and needs me to keep him company before the wind carries his soul to heaven. I remind myself that I don't believe in ghosts and look back down the trail again.

I scream at the path. "You should be ashamed of yourself. How much is enough? You are the Devil's highway. Why do you do this to people? How many lives must you ruin? Are you out to get us? What next? Must we all die? Leave us alone and let us go in peace. I don't know how much more we can take." I feel like the supreme naysayer, Horace Blocker, or the superstitious Oona Reid.

What a ridiculous impulse, to yell at dirt and rocks. They're just words anyway. I'm not sure I believe in the Devil any more than I believe in ghosts. Whether it's luck, fate, or simply being in the wrong place at the wrong time, The Oregon Trail seems like an endless succession of trials, tribulations, and tragedies.

My gaze returns to the big rock that pitched Pious' wagon and caused it to roll over his son. Then I peer closer. Is my mind playing tricks on me? I lean forward as if that will help. It looks like Bacon's painting of Bartholomieux on the face of the tornado, only now, the image appears on the rock's surface. How is such a thing possible? I blink rapidly and focus my eyes on the rock again, but he's still there. I can't look at it any longer.

I glance back in the direction from which we came. In the distance, I see another chain of wagons creeping along the trail. It occurs to me that I should wait and warn them about the spiteful rock and its murderous ways. When I look back at it again, it is just a rock.

Not long ago, I worried that Rose was losing her mind. Now I'm beginning to wonder, what about me? I shake my head, slump into my saddle, and ride Blizzard off the mountain at a slow walk.

I'm in no hurry to catch up with the wagons.

As Reverend Meadows says the burying words, I watch Addie and Pious from the crowd's edge. When they lower the poor boy's severed body into a hole, all I can think is, why? Why did this have to happen? Maybe they should have stayed home.

I glance down the ridiculously named Strawberry Creek and think about the families we traveled with. It's as if each family must make a sacrifice along the way. We lost Larkin. Stillman lost Carter, Esther lost Ellen, Cobb lost Jennie, and now Addie and Pious have lost their youngest child. We're not even halfway to Oregon yet.

Is it fair to blame The Oregon Trail? Why did we ever agree to come along, at the peril of our families? We were warned about the dangers. Boss Wheel told us to turn around and go home. Why didn't we listen to him? Maybe we should blame ourselves for not having an ounce of sense. Then, I think of the spirit of the man who followed us when we left our hometown. Maybe ghosts don't care whether I believe in them.

What if it isn't the trail itself but the ghosts along The Oregon Trail that are out to get us? When everyone goes to bed, I return to Leander's grave. I spread a blanket on the ground and look up into a brilliant full moon that looks close enough to touch. Brightly twinkling stars surround it. The peacefully babbling creek and the bright panorama of the night sky remind me that good and evil often follow parallel paths. I forgive Strawberry Creek for its misleading name and The Oregon Trail for tragedies that aren't its fault.

The lure of excitement and adventure aren't to blame when things go wrong. Why not blame evil spirits instead?

TUESDAY, JUNE 25

ROSE WAKES ME IN the morning with a shake of my foot. She murmurs, "Leander is glad you stayed with him," and then she walks away.

My eyes follow Rose as I climb to my feet. What in the Heavens is she talking about? Is that her way of telling me that I should know better than to sleep outside at night? I just can't make any sense of her. Reflecting on the last couple of months, I remember that she often speaks as if she knows the thoughts of those who have passed on. It is as if she lives within a strange fantasy world. It's frightening, yet she doesn't seem afraid.

Agapito sounds the trumpet as I start back toward camp. The boys crawl from the tent, and I take Dahlia Jane's hand as she climbs down from the wagon. Andrew wishes me a cheerful good morning and tells me that we should reach the halfway point today. "If we can make it past the 8th and 9th crossings of the Sweetwater River, we should be able to reach South Pass by the end of the day. We might even get as far as Pacific Springs." Did this come from the guidebook, or the surveyor? Whether it is in fact precisely half way to Oregon hardly matters. The fact is, it's a long way back and a great distance forward.

I say, "We shall see, Andrew," and give him what I hope is a reassuring, motherly smile as I lead Dahlia Jane to an improvised outhouse, just for ladies.

Andrew makes it sound easy, but I'm sure another long day's march across the Great American Desert will be anything but. As we trudge forth, I reckon the trail seems gentler today than yesterday. Maybe my recovery from the ague has me feeling more optimistic. Perhaps it is my new understanding with the cosmos, but whatever the reason, despite the recent tragedy of a dear friend's loss, I find myself pulled toward the optimism that is more my nature.

When Agapito rides from wagon to wagon and tells us that we have reached South Pass, I am astonished. I expected a more dramatic scene. Instead, there's just more sand and sage. It looks like a lonesome mountain prairie rather than a famous landmark.

Rugged, rocky mountains stand tall to the north, but perhaps they're twenty miles away. To the south, for several days, we have been watching trapezoid-shaped mountains, called Oregon Buttes, that are only tall because everything around them is so flat. They always seemed just beyond reach. Now, we're as close to the table-shaped bluffs as we're going to get, and they provide a dazzling view. Straight ahead, our thin roadway splits the barren plain. South Pass barely looks like a slope, but Agapito assures us that this point divides the continent. All the waterways we've crossed so far wend their way eventually to the Atlantic Ocean. The next creek we reach, and all the rivers and streams to come will find their way to the Pacific Ocean instead.

It seems like we should stop and have a picnic or throw a party, but it is too soon after losing Leander to celebrate anything. I glance to the left and then to the right. Then I follow the processional down the trail. The guides aren't leading the wagons into a circle. There must be more miles to travel before we stop for the day. Andrew was right. We march on, a couple of miles farther, until we finally reach Pacific Springs. I can't remember when water ever tasted so good. We have made it halfway to Oregon.

Back at Bonneville Point, The Viper sits on his mount looking back at the trail which will soon be crawling with emigrants. Some of the earliest travelers may have squeaked past already, but the vast majority of them will not reach this point in the trail for several weeks to come.

A small bird appears, as if from nowhere, and slaps its body against his hat. Then, the avian creature soars into the sky, tittering, as if it were The Viper who crashed into it.

Until last year, The Viper did all the killing. There was plenty of other work for his brothers to do, and they obediently complied. Last year, they successfully separated the last wagon from a chain of travelers. They hadn't anticipated a woman in the back, firing a rifle at them. The sound of her gun alerted her distant, fellow travelers and she managed to flee with her children. The Viper thinks of that wagon and pictures the words painted on its bonnet. "The Terwilligers." The Viper barked an order. "Kill them. Now." Leon and Sloan each fired at the men from the two wagons, and The Radish searched their pockets before others from the wagon train galloped onto the scene. It was all that The Viper, Leon, Sloan, and The Radish could do to get away without catching a bullet. Previously, there had been no witnesses. No survivors. That time, the woman who fired on them survived, along with who knows how many young'uns she had in her wagon. After that incident, the brothers were more careful to discuss their plans and efficiently execute their victims without alerting others. Whenever possible, the brothers made their crimes look like they had been committed by Indians.

The Viper had hoped to prevent his brothers from having to kill anybody. Now, only The Radish can say that he hasn't killed a man. The youth is far from innocent, often begging his brothers to let him have one of the women. The Radish doesn't beg to be allowed to kill anyone, and he doesn't often beg his brothers to show mercy. It doesn't cross The Viper's mind to wonder what his brothers think of that part of their job. He frowns at the thought, and tries to convince himself that it is time for The Radish to make a kill. It would make it harder for the kid to ride off if his hands were bloodied too, but The Viper can't bear to let the kid take a life.

Since their close call the previous year, The Viper constantly worries about making another such mistake. Confound those Terwilligers. His brothers are sick of hearing about the incident. Before each of their attacks, The Viper talks about every scenario that could be imagined so that they have a plan for any eventuality. The Viper always finishes these discussions by saying, "That must never happen again."

At Bonneville Point, The Viper tells himself it will not be long now. With any luck, after this year, he and his brothers can retire. Then, his brothers will be happy. But their idea of happiness sounds awful to The Viper. The thought of living lavishly with a servant always underfoot makes him want to spit. The Viper can't stand to be crowded.

WEDNESDAY, JUNE 26

BEFORE DEPARTING CAMP THIS morning, we gather at The Hub and debate a gut-wrenching choice. The wagon master explains the trail. "The Sublette Cutoff could shave forty-six miles off our journey. It is a shortcut."

It's tempting to eliminate more than two long days of marching, but in the final analysis, what difference does it make if it takes us 177 or 180 days to complete our voyage? I suppose if a blizzard catches us in the mountains a day or two short of our goal, we'll wish we had taken the alternate route.

Boss Wheel continues, "On the other hand, taking the Sublette Cutoff requires us to march fifty miles between sources of drinkable water. The only way to survive this barren stretch of desert is to fill the kegs before setting out, and travel throughout the night between two long, strenuous days."

Agapito warns, "Everyone is afraid of the bandidos, yes? Maybe with good reason. But the shortcut has killed hundreds more men, women, and children than the outlaws have. Think about that, mis amigos."

Incredibly, half of the travelers still advocate taking the shortcut. Those of us who don't have enough food appeal to the others. I beg, "We're running

short of supplies. We'll starve if we don't get provisions at Fort Bridger."
For once, I am glad that Captain Meadows has the authority to decide for
all of us. Galusha Gains and others are angry at the decision and threaten
to cross the desert on their own. Boss Wheel promises them they will be
sorry. I wonder how far away the fork in the road is.

Finally, as the sun comes up, we start our travel day. The endless trail
often gives the mind plenty of time to ruminate. Usually, my better nature
prevails, but today, my thoughts are mired in gloominess.

We pass a remarkable landmark called Plume Rocks, resembling a giant,
upside-down waterfall made of rock. So glum, I march past without giving
the natural wonder its due, unaware of how long we've been on the trail
today. Probably hours will pass before our midday stop for dinner.

I still can't get over the loss of Pious and Addie's son, Leander. Pious,
Noah, Larkin and I were schoolmates. I knew Pious' parents and grandparents well. Leander is named after his great-grandfather, a testament to
the family's long history in our hometown which barely touched the edges
of the civilized world. We were surrounded by unexplored mountains, yet
it was a part of the United States of America. The men who worked at
felling trees and floating them to market had dangerous jobs. Our town
knew its share of tragedies. Last year, a man was crushed in the river, leaving
his young wife a widow and their unborn child fatherless. Alas, the poor
woman was one of Bartholomieux's conquests, but that's another matter.

The dangers of living at the edge of civilization are harsh enough. This
unorganized territory is devoid of cities, towns, and hamlets. We're entirely
on our own, aside from a couple of crude buildings that surround distant
forts. Beyond that, there are only a couple of soldiers, here and there, to
protect us. At this point, we've lost so many friends and family members

that it would hardly surprise me to see a giant, wing-flapping, fire-breathing dragon swoop down and incinerate us all. Every loss we experience along The Oregon Trail is a tragedy. Thinking about the people who have needlessly died along the way twists my gut until the next death hits me harder still. It's bad enough when an adult dies, but there's something about the death of a child that's impossible to overcome.

By late morning, I realize that I've been fixated on my feet for so long that I don't remember how long my brain has been devoid of thought. I look about me, and everyone else seems preoccupied as well. Finally, we reach the Dry Sandy River. Except for intermittent pools of questionable water, the stream is empty. After a short rest and a long drink from our kegs, we resume our march.

In the middle of the afternoon, we reach the point that I have dreaded. The path to the right is hardly faint. It's plain to see that many people who have traveled with other wagon trains have decided to make the big gamble. The way to the left leads southwest rather than due west and is more pronounced. It is evident that far more people opt for the safer route. I close my eyes and pray that everyone travels together rather than splitting up.

The wagons stop briefly in front of the fork in the trail. The view in each direction is identical. If it weren't for the experience of our guides, we'd have no way of knowing where these trails lead. We have reached the point where everyone must decide. Agapito blows his horn, and the wagons begin to move. My head turns to the right as we plod down the trail, watching to see if anyone strikes off on their own. We'll never know whose life was saved by making the decisions we have. What gut-wrenching losses have we avoided? If we made the opposite decision, what perils would we have faced? I've been curious about Fort Bridger and despite the nearly fifty extra miles, it makes me glad to know we're going to get to visit civilization, albeit briefly.

I can't think about the Parting of the Ways any longer. With a few words to Stillman and the children, I walk back three wagons to visit Addie and Pious. I don't stay long. There's nothing I can say to make them feel better. All I can do is let them know that they're not alone.

When we reach today's destination, I want to collapse. It's been days since deciding that I was cured of the ague, but by the end of a long day's journey, I'm not so sure. At least there is water in the Little Sandy River.

THURSDAY, JUNE 27

WHEN I MAKE MY way back to the Bull's wagon again, Addie says, "Thank you for coming, Dorcas. I don't know what I'd do without you."

"I just wish there was something I could do or say, dear."

"I know. Even if you didn't say two words all afternoon, it makes me feel better just having you here."

I take Addie's hand in mine and walk for a few minutes, just holding her hand. After a couple of minutes, she drops my hand, turns to me, and says, "Do you think we'll make it to Oregon?"

Hopefully, my words don't sound forced. It's important that my statement sounds reassuring. Without hesitation, I say, "I do," yet I feel a twinge inside. I'm not sure whether I'm saying so to make her feel better or whether I really believe my own words. I never begin a day thinking, this is the day something terrible will happen and we're all going to die. Yet only yesterday, I conjured up a fire-breathing dragon, as if there aren't enough disasters that have plagued our journey.

Addie speaks, saying a couple of words quickly, then a couple of words slowly. She talks like she walks, as if running toward things and away from them at the same time. She laments, "I can't remember why we decided to go to Oregon. We were perfectly content, and then one day, everybody was talking about free land. Then, suddenly, it seemed like we got swept into the commotion of making plans to go too. If only we had stayed at home, I'd still have my baby."

"I know, dear. It is hard to look back and wish things had turned out differently."

Addie says, "I don't know how you get on without Larkin. I don't know what I'd do if anything happened to Pious." She gulps and stifles a sob as if grieving the loss of her husband as well as her child.

I look at my friend and say, "Some days, it hardly seems real. It's almost as if I expect to turn around and see Larkin curling his mustache between his fingers. Other days, it feels like he has been gone for years. It helps to have Stillman traveling with us. He has been a godsend."

Addie reaches over and taps me on the arm. Then, she reminds me of every death and tragedy we've suffered, from Bridget Sawyer to poor Leander and everyone in between, including the family of four from another wagon train that burned in the grassfire. Walking with Addie makes me blue, but if I'm honest with myself, I'm not in the mood to be cheerful today.

My mind wanders in and out of the conversation as Addie paints a picture of Leander apprenticing to Larkin. I think back to the day Leander asked me to teach him how to open the safe before we left it to rust at Red Buttes. It is sad to think about the wasted potential of dreams that never had a chance to come true. Addie says, "I like to picture them working together, giving people advice about their money, and protecting them from financial ruin by placing their savings in the vault." She looks at me pleadingly, as if I have the power to turn back the hands of time, and grant her son an apprenticeship to my husband.

As a deep breath of air expands my lungs, I recall the past. There was always a contented expression on Larkin's face as he made entries in the journal at the inn in our hometown. He enjoyed keeping the books and updating the ledgers. He always said that without meticulous attention to detail, there was no hope of the owner of the inn turning a profit. I tell Addie, "I can almost see it in my mind."

She says, "Every day when I think of my baby, I am going to imagine him greeting depositors and counting money. It will make me proud thinking that he's helping everybody keep their hard earned money safe."

I verbalize acknowledgement, murmuring, "Mm–hmm." When someone experiences a tragic loss, most people think it is better not to mention lost loved ones. Maybe some folks feel differently, but I prefer to think of Larkin rather than pretend he never existed, just as Charlotte tries to keep her son Martin alive by talking about him frequently.

In an animated voice, Addie imagines all of the terrible things that could still happen to us. It is hard to imagine there is any hazard that hasn't yet confronted us, but Addie has a creative imagination when it comes to all the things that could go wrong. I suppose a volcano could rise from the desert floor in front of us. I frown when she speaks of outlaws and wolves. If she doesn't stop, I'm going to start talking about that fire-breathing dragon.

I glance at Addie. Despite the miles, and the fact that she is almost forty years old, the woman looks as pretty as a young bride. Her straight, blond hair neatly frames her face and doesn't stray from the confines of her sunbonnet. Her skin is pale, and her complexion is clear. It's as if the elements haven't found their way beneath the protection of her bonnet. A woman of forty should have at least a touch of frown lines, laugh lines, or crow's feet. Though we have marched thousands of miles since we left our hometown and deprived ourselves of desserts most days, her figure remains full, and her black spotted dress is clean and unfaded. How does she do it?

The grieving woman looks as fresh as a springtime flower, and I feel like a sunflower after the first kiss of frost. Thank heavens we've arrived at the Big Sandy River. It looks like more of a stream than a river to me, but it's good to put another day of travel behind us.

When I return to our wagon, Andrew tells us that we have marched twenty miles today. "Mr. Franzwa said so." I think of the strange looking man with half a beard and bear-like feet, and shake my head as if trying to expel the image from my mind. I should help the children settle into camp, but I'm weary. I feel like I have the ague again. Dr. Appleyard warned me of the after-effects, but I didn't believe him.

I do now.

Friday, June 28

Our guides have let us sleep late this morning. When the trumpet sounds at dawn, I glance about and see that Rose is already up and gone. She often rises before Reveille, but I become concerned when Rose fails to materialize as the boys and I prepare for our morning departure.

After harnessing the oxen, I can no longer wait patiently for my daughter to appear. I hate asking for help, but when it comes to a child's safety, one cannot be too proud. Our guides are finishing their breakfast at the wagon master's camp when I sound the alarm. It's rare to find Boss Wheel, Agapito, Arikta, and Dembi Koofai all in camp at the same time. I exclaim, "Rose is missing!"

I can't bear to look at Boss Wheel. The gruff ramrod has made his feelings about Rose crystal clear. Agapito tells the scouts to fetch the horses as the wagon master cusses in French. Then, ever so briefly, Agapito places a reassuring hand on my shoulder.

Dembi Koofai returns at a fast trot, with Arikta right behind him. The Shoshone says, "Rio is missing." He says more with his hands than with the words he speaks. "I track."

Agapito fills in the missing details, though I know enough of the hand talk to understand that Dembi Koofai thinks Rose is riding Rio. There are no other tracks, so whatever has happened, kidnapping and horse thievery are not suspected. It appears that Rose has ridden off on the assistant wagon master's horse alone and on purpose.

Agapito tells Dembi Koofai and Arikta to follow the missing horse's trail, but Boss Wheel interrupts him. "The wagons will continue. I'll ride point, Arikta will ride drag, and you stay with the wagon. Dembi Koofai can go alone."

I say, "I'm going with him." Agapito's brow furrows and he shakes his head slowly. He looks concerned but I can't worry about that now.

Boss Wheel scowls at me. "I don't recommend it. This is Shoshone country." His scowl deepens into a sneer. "Dembi Koofai can move faster on his own without having to look out for you. He knows the country, and he is our best tracker." Boss Wheel turns his back to me and tells his scout, "We will camp on the Big Sandy tonight and the Green River the next two nights."

I don't care what Boss Wheel says. I'm going with Dembi Koofai. I turn my back and run toward camp. After a few quick words with Stillman and the children, I saddle Blizzard, fill a canteen, and toss biscuits in my saddlebags. Andrew looks confused, Christopher appears jealous, and Dahlia Jane seems like she wants to cry. I try to reassure them. "Don't worry, children, we'll find your sister."

Dahlia Jane says, "What if something happens to *you*, Mama?" The child bursts into tears, and I can't imagine what tragedy she imagines. There isn't time for more, so I hug her quickly and promise her that there is no need to worry. I can feel my face twitching as I say words to the child that I can't possibly be sure of myself.

Dembi Koofai has a lead on me, but Blizzard catches up quickly. He rides along at a fast trot, eyes following a dusty trail that is so clear, even I could follow it.

I ask, "How do you know it's Rio and Rose's trail."

"Ever' horse is differen'. They don' go fas'."

"How old are the tracks?" If Rose rode off in the last hour or so, we should find her fast.

"Don' know." The mysterious scout doesn't offer suspicions, voice concerns, or express worry. I imagine tracking takes concentration, so I fall back a little and let the man do his work.

Soon after, Dembi Koofai turns back to me and says, "They go fas'." He turns back and follows the straight trail in a southeastern direction. I watch the constellations of spots strewn across his horse's speckled haunches as the Shoshone rides at a spirited, mile-eating trot.

We maintain a steady pace without stopping to rest. My throat is parched, and I need a drink, but I appreciate the scout's diligence. My daughter's life could depend on finding her quickly. There is no time to stop. We shall tend to our thirst later.

After hours on the flat trail, we reach an area of rocky hills, and beyond them lies a ridge of mountains. Dembi Koofai doesn't appear to be watching the ground as much. Instead, he looks toward the mountains in the distance as if hoping to see movement on the horizon. It's been hours since he has spoken. Finally, he turns to me, points, and says, "I know where she goin'."

Rose doesn't ride horses that often, and I can't remember her ever riding bareback. I don't know why she would think she could take a horse that doesn't belong to us. We've been trailing her all day. She must have ridden off in the middle of the night, or we would have caught up to her hours ago. What's gotten into that child now?

An hour later, the Shoshone says, "Almos' there."

The distant gray mountains seem to have changed color now that we're in them. An impressive rise of yellow and brown sandstone stands tall above us as we ride toward it. A trickle of smoke leads from somewhere on the other side of the prominence. Before we circle around the bluff, Dembi Koofai says, "We are not alone. Don' worry." He makes the sign for friends and then the sign for family. I can't fathom how he could know. Perhaps he has seen more tracks or other evidence.

We continue at a slow walk. A couple of minutes later, the solemn scout coughs quietly at first and then louder. I've never heard the man make such a sound before. The horses take a couple more steps, and I see Rose seated beside a fire with a small group of Indians: two middle-aged men, a younger woman heavy with child, and a couple of children. I gasp at the sight of my missing daughter, surprised to see her sitting with strangers, and relieved that she appears unharmed.

I glance to the left and see Rio, the horse that Rose borrowed without permission, standing at rest in the shade of a steep rock wall. I squint and see crude pictures scratched into the brown sandstone. They are a curiosity. If only there were time to look at them.

In front of me, Dembi Koofai slides from Coffeepot's back and approaches the fire. I also dismount.

The men rise, and Dembi Koofai greets the taller man. Instead of shaking hands, the men clasp each other's forearms near the bend of their elbows. The shorter man has a hunched back and scary-looking, white eyes. After exchanging a few words with Dembi Koofai, the short man sits across from Rose and stares into her face.

I step toward Dembi Koofai and the taller man, and peek at Rose, who doesn't acknowledge my arrival. She sits cross-legged and silently stares into the strange man's haunting gaze.

Dembi Koofai turns halfway toward me, not turning his back toward the taller man. "This man Chief Washakie. Ver' good friend." Then Dembi Koofai walks backward toward the horses and crouches in the shade beside his Appaloosa.

I don't know how to greet this man. Should I offer my hand or try to grasp his arm as Dembi Koofai did? Not knowing what else to do, I curtsy and admonish myself. Chief Washakie looks at my legs. He must have seen Larkin's trousers. Then, he looks at my bosom, smiles, and looks into my eyes. By now, I should be accustomed to the way men's eyes linger when they look at my chest. I know better than to wait for the scout to introduce me, especially given the fact that he has stepped away from Chief Washakie. My tongue trips as I try to speak, and I eventually spit my name into the air. The warm, friendly smile on the Chief's round cheeks puts me at ease.

Washakie reaches his hand toward me like a southern gentleman. I extend my hand, and he takes it into his. He bows softly toward me, his straight black hair cascading over his shoulders.

"It is nice to meet you, Dorcas. Is this child your daughter? You must be very proud."

I glance at Rose, who doesn't seem to be listening to me and the chief. "Yes, Chief. Her name is Rose Moon. I'm so relieved that we found her. I was very worried."

He looks at me with sympathetic eyes. "You need not worry about this one." He sweeps an arm toward Rose as if casting a spell of invincibility upon her. "The ancient ones watch over her. But a mother always worries about her children." He turns toward the woman who stands a short distance away and speaks to me. "Would you like to meet my wife?"

I'm distracted by the Indian's words. What ancient ones? How could they watch over Rose? Sometimes it seems like the whole world is going mad. I say, "Yes, Chief. It would be an honor, your Highness." I don't know how to talk to an Indian chief, and I hope I'm doing so correctly.

"Please call me Washakie. Should I call you Mrs. Moon?"

"Thank you, Washakie. That is most kind. You may call me Dorcas."

Washakie beckons the Indian woman with his hand, and she steps toward us. "This is Crimson Dawn, and these are our youngest children."

I extend my hand. Forgetting to be ladylike, I realize that my grip is too firm. I relax my hand, and Crimson Dawn bows her head toward me as she brings her hand back to her side. I'm surprised when she says, "You are like the woman who left her handprints in stone." She points at a nearby rock.

Washakie extends an arm toward the rock and suggests we take a closer look. "This is the Birthing Stone. Crimson Dawn hopes to have the baby here, but the little one doesn't seem to be in a hurry."

I can't believe I'm in the presence of an Indian chief, let alone talking with him about childbirth. He seems to be at ease. I think of Boss Wheel and Captain Meadows, who are nothing like this man. Perhaps being away from the responsibility of leadership causes Washakie to be relaxed. The coming birth of a child doesn't seem to unnerve him either. I wonder how many children he has fathered, and then I try to estimate his age.

As if reading my mind, the man looks at me and says, "You are trying to guess my age. The truth is, only the Great Spirit knows for sure. I was orphaned young, but I've seen at least forty winters. What about you, Dorcas?"

"A lady never reveals her true age." I grin. "But I am happy to confide in you, Washakie. I am thirty-four."

The chief leads us from the Birthing Stone to the wall that shades the horses. I think of the names, initials, and years carved into Independence Rock and other places along the dusty roadway we have traveled. The ancient drawings on these remote mountains make me think differently about leaving something for future people to wonder about.

One illustration features a long horse carrying a stick figure with an impressive array of feathers flowing down his back. The oversized spear with a point half as large as the rider seems to have an oval aura surrounding it. I try to imagine the warrior or hunter preserving his likeness in stone, patiently scratching away at the soft rock for hours. I think of Bacon and try to imagine an ancient Indian, eons ago, preserving a single moment in stone.

The wall features many pictures of buffalo. Some are more intricate than others and require an active imagination to see. Many images look like feet. From their shape, I don't think they represent people. They look more like bear footprints to me.

The most curious images I see are of one animal drawn inside another. I look back at the Birthing Stone, standing in the bright afternoon sun a short distance away. Then, I look at an etching that appears to show an animal giving birth. I gasp at the next symbol I see. At the risk of sounding vulgar, the only way I can think to describe it is to say it looks like an unmentionable lady part. Despite the depiction of a hunter with a huge spear, this sacred landmark seems like a place dedicated to womanhood.

Next, Washakie leads us into the shade. He says, "This is a sacred place of life, fertility, and rebirth." I wonder what he means by rebirth. Does he refer to a spiritual reawakening of some sort? There is a feeling of optimism that overwhelms me.

I look at the wise chief and say, "This is a very special place."

"Would you spend the night as our guests, Dorcas?"

I look away for a moment. It took us so long to get here, there's no chance of returning to The Oregon Trail tonight. I look back and say, "Thank you, Washakie. We'd be much obliged."

When we return to the small fire, Crimson Dawn hands me a bowl of stew. Washakie's friend sits like a statue and continues looking into Rose's face, and she stares back with that same vacant expression that always scares me.

I don't know what to say about my daughter's strange behavior. I want to jostle her and force her to acknowledge my presence, but experience has taught me not to disturb her during such moments. Instead, I say to Washakie. "Sometimes, my daughter seems asleep and awake at the same time."

Washakie looks at me knowingly. He says, "Do not worry, Dorcas. I understand." I scratch my chin as he speaks, and look at Rose. I wish I could say that I understand.

As I slowly chew the thick stew, Washakie tells me that his friend is known as Sees Through Clouds. I ask if the man is blind, and Washakie says his vision comes and goes. "Like many who lose their vision, Sees Through Clouds can see things that others cannot. His medicine is very strong."

After a moment passes, I decide to ask a question. I understand why Washakie and his wife have come to this place. I'm surprised that another woman hasn't come along to help Crimson Dawn during her confinement. But, I don't understand the presence of the medicine man. Afraid of offending, I whisper to the chief, "Why is Sees Through Clouds here?"

Washakie seems to be surprised by my question. "Spirit people are always drawn to sacred places. You know that, Dorcas."

I gulp, wanting to inquire further but unable to speak the words: *Do I?*

After a delicious meal and great conversation with the chief and his pleasant wife, I'm weary and ready to retire. Everyone is quiet, and I'm expecting Washakie to suggest that everyone go to bed.

Dembi Koofai sits beside me but slightly away from the fire. He's been quiet as usual. Sometimes, I turn my head and glance at him just to see if he's still here.

Since we arrived, Rose's vacant fog lifted sufficiently to tend to basic biological necessities. I tried to speak to her when I led her away, but she neither acknowledged my presence nor indicated she knew I was speaking. When she ate, she chewed like she was matching the slow rhythm of native drums. The most unnerving thing to witness as her mother is the strange countenance of the man, Sees Through Clouds, who seems to be out of his head as much as she is. Over the past several months, Rose's strange ways have become more and more concerning. Though I hate to admit it, I may have to accept that Rose will never be her old self again.

When Dembi Koofai suddenly bounds forward, chattering in his native language, I wince. He holds a scorpion in his hand. Over and over again, the rickety spider unfurls its curly tail and strikes his hand. Dembi Koofai giggles and laughs like someone is tickling him. The mysterious scout with the mystical countenance seems like a different person as he rejoices in being stung repeatedly by the devilish creature. When the scorpion's energy wanes, Dembi Koofai holds the spider over his naked chest. The arachnid lashes out with its claws and grabs hold of Dembi Koofai's skin, tightly clamping its tiny pincers into the Shoshone's naked flesh.

The young man, who always looks like he wants to disappear, smiles proudly, thrusts his chest forward, boastfully and looks down at the insect that clings to him like an adornment. I've never witnessed anything like what just happened, and can't stop looking at the young man's chest. The scorpion looks like it clings to life as it clutches Dembi Koofai. Perhaps it perished after latching on. The scout speaks to Washakie. "I'll stand watch."

Our host says, "Wake me when you are tired."

When Dembi Koofai is gone, I tell Washakie that the scout regards the scorpion as his spirit creature. If I live to be a hundred, I'll never forget moments like this. My chest heaves with exhilaration. I've been told that scorpions aren't lethal this far north, but something about watching the scout's brave display seemed dangerous. A year ago, I never imagined that I'd be camping in a sacred location with scorpions and an Indian chief.

Washakie says, "Scorpions are masculine symbols of youthfulness, potency, and vigor. Their presence here, at this monument to womanhood, represents balance."

SATURDAY, JUNE 29

IN THE MORNING, I feel refreshed in a way that I haven't felt in a long time. It is as if I slept for days. I'm glad to finally have the after-effects of the fever and ague behind me. I remember Washakie telling me that this is a place of *rebirth*. I wonder if he believes in reincarnation or whether he speaks of rejuvenation. I don't believe in the former but don't deny the latter.

I yawn and rub my eyes, excited to face a new day. Daylight colors the horizon. When I look around, I notice that I'm alone, except for Dembi Koofai, who lies sleeping on his back, barely visible in a dark cranny where rock meets dirt.

As I step around a rock and into the day, early morning sunshine floods my face. Crimson Dawn hands me a cup of coffee beside the fire. I'm surprised, and say, "Good morning. I didn't know that Indians drank coffee." I cover my mouth with my free hand. It seems like such a foolish thing to say. Sometimes, I don't think before speaking.

Crimson Dawn smiles and says, "We like it."

Washakie says, "You can blame the mountain men. My friend Jim Bridger got me hooked on the stuff."

Dembi Koofai silently appears. The quiet man adds, "Is ver' good." I look at his chest as he rubs his eyes. The crusty spider's lifeless exoskeleton still clings to his skin. The scout must have slept throughout the night on his back without rolling over. With coffee in hand, he retreats to the company of his horse.

Rose sits with her back to the medicine man, frozen like a statue. I can't help thinking that both of them have gone thoroughly loco. Larkin said that Rose would outgrow it, but now that I've encountered Sees Through Clouds, I'm not so sure.

Sometimes it is hard to say goodbye to new friends, even those we've only known for a short time. It's particularly difficult to part ways with Washakie and Crimson Dawn. It would be wonderful to travel with them, but I'm glad to leave Sees Through Clouds behind. Whether Rose wishes to leave or not, it is time to return to the wagon train.

Dembi Koofai brings the horses, helps Rose mount Rio, and hands me a lead rope to ensure that she follows me on Blizzard. We set out into the desert, and I turn back and wave. Then, I follow Dembi Koofai along a scant trail headed due west.

As the hours go by, Rose becomes more and more lucid. She doesn't question why we're here, mention where we've been, or speak of our experience, but at least she seems to be present in the moment. I'm glad she's making her way back to sanity. Under the scorching desert sun, I shiver at the thought that one of these days, she may not return. I wonder whether Washakie's medicine man has experienced the same transformation as Rose.

Late afternoon, Dembi Koofai leads us into a canyon. It feels like we're hidden within a crack, and I imagine that suits the elusive scout. After an hour, I spy movement far ahead. I squeeze my legs slightly, urging Blizzard forward, and whisper to Dembi Koofai. "What do you see?"

"Wild horses."

"Oh," I can barely contain myself. "Mustangs? Can we ride among them? Do you think I could throw a loop over one?"

"Can try. Ver' hard."

"Can they be tamed?"

"Can try. Not ever' mustang can." He shrugs. I don't know whether he's trying to convey uncertainty or doesn't have the words to explain what he's thinking.

"I understand, Dembi Koofai. I want to try. It will be up to the Great Spirit to decide whether I can catch one."

"Yes, we try." When he says *try*, it sounds more like *dry*.

I make the hand signal Arikta taught me for *horse*, and he rewards me with a rare smile as he returns the sign. He reaches for the lead rope. "I lead Rose."

I nod and spirit Blizzard into a fast walk. As we move forward, I untie the lariat from my saddle and drape it over the horn. If I must gallop into a moving herd, I'll have a chance to lasso a mustang, but my odds will be greater if we can slowly merge into the herd and lazily rope a horse while it grazes. Wild animals are skittish. I glance back at Dembi Koofai and reckon he has a wild spirit as well. The more time I spend west of Independence, the more I can identify with that.

As we get closer, Dembi Koofai tells me to let our horses eat. He thinks if the wild herd sees our horses grazing, we're more likely to infiltrate the herd.

Miraculously, it works.

Blood pounds through my veins as I pretend to be calm and relaxed. A gorgeous paint horse with wild eyes, a long body, and a short, unnaturally arched neck attracts my attention. It seems like a ridiculous thought, but the big mare reminds me of myself. She also reminds me of the long horse I saw yesterday on the sacred wall. I decide to see if I can catch her and nudge Blizzard in her direction. The mare tosses her disheveled mane, snorts, and approaches curiously.

The stocky Andalusian seems as taken with the mustang mare as I am and sidles up toward her. I'll never have a better chance to capture a wild horse. My right hand rests near the saddle horn, and the paint horse's head turns slightly, exposing the perfect opportunity to drop a rope over her head. The instant I have the mustang roped, Blizzard begins backing up. I barely have time to wrap the rope around the horn before the wild mare rears and paws the ground before her, as if trying to attack the rope.

The rest of the herd stampedes up the hillside as the roped horse pounds the ground. It seems like the horse's vision is impaired. It is as if it is trying to see the object it feels on its neck, and at the same time, I can feel its gaze upon Blizzard and me. I speak to her in what I hope is a reassuring voice and let up slightly on the tension in the rope.

I walk Blizzard past the mare, leaving the rope somewhat slack. It is surprising how quickly the lanky mustang falls in. Looking at her takes my breath away. I'm amazed to have captured her. What good fortune. Can she be tamed? For now, she seems content to walk beside us.

When Dembi Koofai gets close enough to talk to him, I say, "I'd like to name her after you."

He says his own name, but the look on his face seems confused. "Dembi Koofai?"

"No. Not exactly. How do Shoshone say scorpion?"

For the second time in as many days, the stone-faced scout flashes his brilliant white teeth and a proud grin. Otherwise, he rarely smiles. He says, "*Gwibunzi.*"

I repeat the word back to him as best I can. "Do you mind if I call this horse, Gwibunzi?"

He nods and repeats the name. I'm not sure if he is affirming my pronunciation or correcting me. Either way, I'll do my best to say it properly. Whenever I think about her name, I'll think about my friend, the evanescent scout, and the brazen scorpion ritual he performed.

Throughout the day, we maintain a steady pace. When the afternoon fades into early evening, Dembi Koofai stops and dismounts at a low point in the canyon. He walks a short distance, searching for something, then squats and picks up a flat stone. On his knees, he digs vigorously, burrowing into the sandy soil. When he reaches a depth of about two feet, he clears sand from the rim. He looks up at me and I dismount.

When I look into Dembi Koofai's hole, I see water seeping into it. I look at him and nod.

He says, "Ver' good." His hand makes the sign for water. After a quick trip to his horse's side, he returns with a shallow tin cup from his saddlebag, scoops a little water, and offers it to me. I take a sip, thank him, and pass the cup to Rose.

The biscuits I brought aren't as fresh as I'd like, but they'll do since we're hungry, and there isn't anything else. My stomach grumbles as I pass them around. I volunteer to take watch for the first half of the night and pray that it doesn't rain as Rose and Dembi Koofai stretch out on the ground and go to sleep.

As I pace the canyon to ensure I don't fall asleep, the phrase Widow Moon crosses my mind. As I look at Gwibunzi in the moonlight, I consider a new name for myself. Mustang Moon comes to mind, and I nod into the oblivious canyon.

SUNDAY, JUNE 30

I'M STILL TURNING THE phrase "Mustang Moon" in my head and quietly on my tongue despite the blazing heat of the mid-afternoon sun. The words please me. The wild-looking, spotted horse at the end of my lead rope makes me feel like my secret nickname, Mustang Moon, is justified.

The horses lift their legs high, pulling their hooves from the boggy sand as we splash across the shallow, flat-bottomed stream known generously as the Big Sandy River. I'm looking forward to reuniting with our fellow travelers after a couple of days of separation. So much has happened. It's hard to believe that we've only been away for a couple of days.

A short distance later, we reach the wild, fast-moving Green River. I thought that our group of nomads would be wiling away the afternoon, safely on the other side. Instead, we find them lined up near a ferry landing on the east side of the river.

I call out to Stillman and the children as we ride up. I expected them to be glad to see us. The oxen stomp their feet and switch their rangy tails about behind them. I look up and down the line of waiting travelers. Even from a distance, everyone looks irritated. It's not just my family.

Dembi Koofai gracefully slides from the back of the black Appaloosa. The scout lands beside Stillman, whose head leans forward. His eyes widen, and he stares unblinkingly at the Shoshone's chest. I can only imagine his thoughts, knowing his distaste for spiders, but it looks like he's shocked rather than fearful or horrified.

Andrew scowls, steps forward, and takes Blizzard's reins as I drop to the ground and turn toward Stillman and Dembi Koofai. Stillman's head rises slowly, and he looks directly into Dembi Koofai's eyes as the guide proudly puffs his chest forward. Stillman's mouth hangs open in wide amazement. Then he looks back at the scorpion corpse dangling precariously from Dembi Koofai's pinched skin.

Rose scoffs and slides from Rio, landing with a thud. Dembi Koofai turns away from Stillman. Dutifully, he leads Coffeepot and Rio to Boss Wheel's wagon.

Christopher groans and Dahlia Jane holds her arms up. I lift my child into my arms and rub her back. "I told you we'd be alright, darling."

Stillman takes Gwibunzi's lead rope absentmindedly. His gaze follows the departing Indian, and his head shakes slowly from side to side. He doesn't say anything, but I can almost hear him saying, "Don't that beat all you ever saw?"

Christopher lifts his upper lip and says, "What's with the spotted horse?"

Stillman looks at the lanky paint horse and turns to me. He gulps hard and says, "And what about the scorpion?"

Rose wanders around to the back of the wagon as I tell Stillman, Andrew, and Christopher about the last couple of days. Stillman squeezes his eyes closed, and his face pinches up when I get to the part about the scorpion. Andrew nods curiously when I talk about Washakie and the sacred stone. In his head, he's probably practicing the words that he'll post in *The Times*. Christopher looks impressed when I tell them about catching Gwibunzi. Before I finish, he asks, "Can I ride her?"

"Maybe after she's tamed and when your broken arm heals."

He looks down at his arm in its sling and says, "I forgot about that." A sneer forms on his upper lip.

Andrew explains that they've been waiting all day to cross. "It's eight dollars to cross, and that's just for the wagon. We have to swim the stock across. Yesterday it was five dollars, but there were several wagon trains ahead of us." He points to the waiting wagon trains behind us and says, "When these folks showed up, the ferryman said that price depends on demand."

Finally, it's our turn to cross. The slow-moving ferry transports us across the wide river, and we're lucky to make it to the other side today. After we settle into camp, Cobb wanders over from the next wagon to get a closer look at the mustang.

I reach for baby Jenny, and Cobb gives me a quick nod. Then he turns to Gwibunzi. The gentle man caresses the wild mare's short, curved neck. He sings to her in a low voice as his hands glide gently across her withers. Gwibunzi turns her head slowly to watch him, and Cobb slowly reaches an open hand toward her face. The horse separates her lips and muzzles Cobb's palm. She lowers her head, and Cobb stokes the lightning bolt-shaped blaze that zigzags from her forelock to her muzzle.

I say, "She hardly seems like a wild horse anymore," as Cobb scratches behind her ears. He opens his mouth to say something, but doesn't get the chance.

I'm startled by a voice behind me. "What a hideous beast," says Captain Meadows.

My head juts forward. "What do you mean?" I've never seen a horse that looks more like a work of art. "Why do you say that?"

Captain Meadows' nose turns red and his cheeks shake as he says, "Wild horses are vermin. You can see the devil in that misfit's eye. Mustangs can't be trusted. They should be hunted and exterminated."

Galusha appears beside the preacher. "Want me to shoot it?" The hunter looks directly at Cobb rather than at the beautiful mustang mare.

I pass Jenny back to Cobb and take the lead rope from my friend. Then I turn to Captain Meadows. "She has a wild heart and a loving spirit. Gwibunzi is an angel, not a devil. I intend to tame her. Then I plan to breed her."

Captain Meadows shakes his head and frowns. "Such pairings result in magnification of the sire's and dam's worst traits."

Galusha spits on Gwibunzi's foreleg, but the mustang stands.

"With all due respect, Captain, I aim to take my chances."

"I'd rather you get rid of it. I'm not in favor of traveling with wild beasts."

Monday, July 1

It is late in the afternoon after a long day of traveling. At a stream known as the Blacks Fork of the Green River, Cobb and I stand beside Gwibunzi. The sooner she's tamed, the better. I clutch a long, coiled rope tied tightly to her halter in case she gets spooked. Our goal for today is to introduce her to the saddle blanket.

Cobb holds the coarse fabric in front of Gwibunzi's muzzle, and she mouths it with her lips. She seems curious. Cobb digs a handful of oats from his pocket and serves them up on the giant cloth platter. The horse's lips separate, and she skillfully drags the feed into her mouth. Cobb's soothing voice reassures her.

We switch places. Cobb takes the lead rope and gives me the saddle blanket. Following the man's instructions, I fold the blanket in half, and slowly rub Gwibunzi's coat with it. She doesn't seem to mind the object's presence. The blanket touches her jowl, glides along her gullet and the windpipe of her neck. She turns her head slightly so that she can see the blanket at her shoulder, breast, and arm. Next, I run the blanket along her neck and then the crest of her mane down to her withers. She seems to like the attention.

It's as if she enjoys the feel of the blanket as I rub her belly, hip, flank, and rump.

Cobb says, "That a girl. Good job." He could be speaking to me, but I'm rather certain that he's talking to Gwibunzi.

I ask, "Should I rub her legs with the blanket?"

"No, I don't think she's ready for that yet."

"Should we try laying the blanket on her back?"

Cobb hesitates and then says, "I guess we could give it a try."

A crowd has gathered and watches us as we work with the mustang. Even the scouts seem interested in Gwibunzi's training. Arikta and Dembi Koofai are seldom seen together, but both are in camp today. The piebald pinto and Appaloosa seem as curious as the rest of the audience. At the front of the crowd, Bobby and Wayne look like they're having a spirited debate. Knowing those pals, such a conversation could easily escalate to an altercation.

I say to Cobb, "You do it."

Cobb and I trade places again. I don't know what to expect, but grab the long rope tightly. Despite having earned Gwibunzi's confidence, when Cobb drapes the saddle blanket over her back, she tosses her head. When she feels threatened, her unusually white, third eyelid makes her eyes seem wild. Gwibunzi whinnies loudly, and then hightails it like a scared rabbit.

I'm glad I'm wearing gloves. After about half of the thick rope unwinds through my hands. My grip catches hold, and whips my body from the ground. I know I should let go, but I'm afraid to lose Gwibunzi. The mustang drags my tumbling body over the rocky ground. Rough sage tugs at my dress as my body tears through the nettlesome shrubs.

I should have the sense to feel pain, but I'm more concerned with holding on tightly. Finally, I can hold on no longer. The remaining rope slips through my fingers as my body crashes into a boulder, yet all I can think of is that Gwibunzi is gone.

When I try to stand, my aching body protests. I toss my tangled hair from my forehead with my right hand and try to assess my injuries. Arikta's horse comes to a sliding stop a few feet away from me, and the young man effortlessly leaps from Howl's back. The Pawnee scout carefully helps me stand, and hushes me. I realize that I'm speaking incoherently. I don't even know what I'm trying to say. I look at my hands. The gloves are torn, and my skin is ripped.

Dembi Koofai gallops away. It looks as if he's in hot pursuit of Gwibunzi. I turn and look back at Cobb and the spectators. I'm amazed at how far away they seem. I look at Arikta and say, "She dragged me all this way?"

"Yes, ma'am. It looks like you were determined to hold on to that rope."

I say, "Sometimes I do the dumbest things. It's like I don't have a lick of sense." I look down at my shredded dress. Thank goodness I wear Larkin's trousers beneath it. The tattered rags look like the hairs at the end of a cow's tail. "I guess that's the end of this dress."

Arikta says, "Yes, ma'am. I do not have a—" the scout pauses as if searching for how to finish his thought. Then he finishes, "lick of sense either. I would have tried to hold on too. You put up a great fight, Dorcas." He says my name tentatively, as if he doesn't know whether he should, or not, but decides to anyhow.

Agapito's adopted youth helps me mount Howl. I ride quietly as Arikta walks along. Rather than converse, I concentrate on trying to ignore my aches and pains. I hate it when people whine. As long as I don't have broken bones or gaping wounds, what is there to complain about? Instead, I blow a soothing breeze into the tattered palms of my hands.

As we approach the onlookers, I can hear their spirited chatter. Do they think that my hearing has been affected by my ordeal?

Captain Meadows says, "I tried to warn that woman." I can't make out the rest of his remarks, but hear the words *silk purse* and *sow's ear*.

Boss Wheel angrily says, "What next? That Dorcas is dumb as a doornail. I swear, that woman's going to be the death of me."

Bobby says, "I think she's a tough dame."

Wayne seems to agree. "Yeah, you should have seen her bouncing across the prairie. She's tough, alright."

Boss Wheel grunts. "I'll grant you that. Maybe she ain't got brains, but she's got sand."

When I try to dismount, my legs give way beneath me. Arikta and Cobb help me to my feet and escort me back to my wagon. I'm sure I look like a wreck, but after a few steps, I find my feet. My muscles obey my wishes. I try to reassure Stillman and the children that I'll be alright. Tears fill my eyes, and I say, "Gwibunzi is gone."

I climb into the wagon and lie on a pile of soft quilts. I had such high hopes for the wild-hearted mustang. I wipe a tear from my eye and admonish myself for acting like a spoiled child.

Tuesday, July 2

In the morning, I feel like an old woman. I wish the children would leave me alone, but they insist on helping me down from the wagon. With my feet on the ground, I slowly stretch my limbs, assessing the full extent of my aches and pains. I can feel my ribs whenever I take a deep breath. My left side is tender and my right thigh smarts. Gripping anything in my scratched up hands causes me pain.

I make my way slowly to the battered, mud-colored quilt that shields the women's latrine. When I drop Larkin's trousers, I get my first look at the monstrous black and blue mark that covers half of my thigh. When I lay a gentle hand over the bruise, I can feel my cheeks tighten into a grimace. Then, I feel an ache on my left shoulder-blade. Bothersome, certainly, but fortunately my injuries aren't more serious.

There's probably an hour yet before the sun rises. It's hard to see very far in the pre-dawn darkness. As I return to my wagon, I see movement to my right and stop in my tracks. Is it just the regular, daily activity of leading the kine to their harnesses? I squint and peer through the darkness and gasp. The surreptitious Dembi Koofai leads a lanky paint horse toward the wagons. Gwibunzi!

Though it pains me, I quickly shuffle forward. Dembi Koofai has just finished tying the mustang to the back corner of our wagon and is attempting to disappear into the darkness, but I am determined not to let him get away. Sharply, I say his name, and I can tell that the silent young man whose appellation means Stone Face stands as still as a statue. It is as if he hadn't meant to be caught.

I make my way through the darkness and attempt to throw my arms around the young man, but he backs away from me. Perhaps Indians aren't accustomed to hugging, or maybe such closeness wasn't practiced in his family as he was growing up. It's not surprising that the furtive scout avoids such contact. He taps his chest with his left hand. I look down, and the dead scorpion still clings to him by one pincer.

I'm so excited about Gwibunzi, I forgot about the arachnid adornment. Instead, I grip his forearms with both of my hands. I gush words into his face, thanking him for catching the lost mustang.

"Is ver' good. She fas'. I catch her though." I've grown to like it when Dembi Koofai talks. It is unlike any accent I've heard before. I wonder why he doesn't pronounce the letters y or t, and th always sounds like d.

"I'm glad to have her back."

"She has my name. We mus' keep her."

I spend most of the day walking beside Gwibunzi and talking with Dahlia Jane as she hangs over the back of the wagon. In the afternoon, after our dinner break, Andrew pokes his head around the wagon. "We've reached Church Butte, Mama. Come see." Dahlia Jane reaches her hands out from the back of the wagon and shakes her hands, indicating that she would like to be picked up. Andrew helps her climb from the moving wagon, and I follow as he leads us around the wagon.

Andrew tells us what Agapito and Arikta told him. "Some people call it Cathedral Rock, Mama." Breathlessly, he exudes, "Look at the tall spires covered with mounded domes. They look like nuns kneeling in prayer."

The prominence is spectacular. The elements have carved layers of petrified clay and sandstone through the eons. The dramatic columns and deep caves make this landmark look like an ancient, long-abandoned castle. As we make our way closer to the outcropping, the children quickly discover the mountain's ability to echo their words back to them. I tell Andrew, "There's something to write about in *The Times* today."

He shouts, "Hear ye," and the mountain echoes his words back to him. Andrew smiles and suggests that Bacon could draw a quick picture of it for the paper as well.

Amazing landmarks don't replace lost loved ones, but they provide some consolation along the way.

After we make camp, Cobb and his children join us at our fire. Dahlia Jane plays with Bess and Joe, and I hold baby Jenny. This time, Gwibunzi has two ropes tied to her neck, Stillman holds one, and Andrew holds the other. Christopher stands at my side and complains about his broken arm. "I can hold the bronc, Mama."

"I know you can, Christopher. It takes two hands though."

I watch as Cobb covers a bit, the part of the bridle that goes in the horse's mouth, with molasses. Then, he holds his sticky palms before Gwibunzi's muzzle. Her long tongue darts in and out of her mouth. Fortunately, she has a sweet tooth. Cobb sings to her and gently slips the bit between her lips. She's too distracted by the bittersweet blackstrap to notice when Cobb straps the bridle over her head.

Andrew approaches us. "Come along, Mama. Name Rock is right over there. Christopher follows Andrew. Bess, Joe, and Dahlia Jane run after them. I shrug at Cobb and nod at Stillman, who chases after the children. Jenny gurgles from the crook of my arm as Cobb leads Gwibunzi toward the big rock.

I enjoy standing in the cool shade of a long overhang. It crosses my mind that it could let loose and fall on our heads. I'm amazed that after carving names and initials in so many different places along the way, the men and boys still find the need to carve their names here, along the four hundred feet of stone. Perhaps there are other places along the way where men have also left their marks. Instead of scratching names into stone, most names are written in globby tar from the wagons' grease buckets.

I'm just glad that emigrants didn't desecrate the sanctity of the Birthing Stone and the rocks where I met Washakie, Crimson Dawn, and Sees Through Clouds.

Floods of bright orange drench the horizon as the brothers return to their cabin on Birch Creek. The Viper thought he would feel relieved to return to the familiar enclave, but his sick stomach does not let up.

The Radish sweeps mouse dung across the floor and out the door. Sloan wastes no time crawling onto his bunk, eager to retire for the evening. The Viper sits on the porch and rolls a smoke.

When The Radish finishes tidying up, he hangs his hat on a wooden peg and sits on the front porch a few feet from his brother.

The Viper quietly speaks. It's as if he knows his words will disrupt the quiet of a peaceful evening. "It's time to get to work, kid."

The Radish begrudges, "I know."

The Viper's acknowledgment almost sounds sympathetic. "Your heart ain't in it."

"That's a fact." The Radish speaks plainly, until he gets to the last word of his sentence. "I hate wasting time that I could be looking for gold." When he says gold, it sounds like he's picturing an abundance of the precious metal.

The Viper sneers. "What makes you think you'll find anything in that blame mountain?"

The younger brother speaks with insistent optimism. "It's in there. I just know it. I wish I could blow that mountain up and filter through the crumbles. There's gold in that mountain. Just gotta be."

With a scoff, The Viper flips the butt of his cigarette into the darkness beyond the ends of his boots. "You could search a hundred years and not find anything. You're more likely to have the mountain cave in on you than to find a streak of gold. The only sure path to richness passes between the wooden wheels of the lumbering wagons. Every one of them has something in it. There's no guarantee in those stinking mountains. Won't catch me crawling around in the dirt looking for flakes and nuggets."

The Radish says, "Someday, Sloan wants to be a gambler. He says that's the easy way to strike it rich."

"Chancy. Gambling. You gotta have a stake to start, and odds are much greater you lose it all rather than walk away with anything to show for your trouble."

The Radish frowns. "And if you do win, somebody's gonna think you cheated and plug a bullet in your gut. Better to find you a lucky mountain."

"Your mining days are numbered, Radish. The season is changing. It's going to be a bloody season, but then we'll live like kings." The Viper hesitates when he says, "Think you can kill a farmer?"

After a long pause, the younger outlaw tentatively says, "I reckon." More forcefully, he says, "Just don't ask me to shoot a pretty, farmer's daughter." The Radish squirms and chuckles as if he's imagining what he will do when he finally gets a chance to be alone with a woman. After he calms down, and his senses return, he looks toward his brother.

The Viper gazes at The Radish, still as a statue and lost in thought. It is as if he were willing himself not to blink, though it is not intentional. It happens more often than he realizes.

The Radish gulps. After a while, he squeaks, "What do you gotta stare at me like that for? You could melt a fellow's brains." He's quiet for a moment, and then he mumbles, "Quit looking at me like that. It gives me the creeps."

The Viper's head spasms and he shakes his head wildly, blinking fast. He realizes that he has been thinking about The Radish running off with a farmer's daughter. He also recalls imagining The Radish shooting a middle aged man standing beside a mule and holding a pitchfork. The Viper has a sense of having been distracted for a time, but is unsure whether it was a couple of seconds or minutes.

Finally, The Radish speaks again. "What if we get ourselves killed?"

The Viper looks away from his brother and crosses his legs at his ankles. "We ain't been killed yet, kid." He casts his gaze downward. He doesn't like the idea of asking The Radish to kill anybody, but can't figure out why. It doesn't bother him when his other brothers do. Coolly, he concludes, "Harvesting pilgrims is easy."

"What about last year?"

The Viper's jaw tenses. "We learned our lesson. We ain't gonna let that happen again."

WEDNESDAY, JULY 3

I WONDER IF BLIZZARD feels jealous of all the attention paid to Gwibunzi. It seems like a third of the travelers regard her as a curiosity. Another third sees her as Captain Meadows does, a misfit who should be exterminated. The final third sees her strength and beauty.

Walking beside Blizzard as we draw nearer to Fort Bridger, the spectacular Uinta mountains rise ahead of us. Dahlia Jane sits on top of the Andalusian stallion, who allows her to ride him as long as I'm nearby. After trudging through arid territory for so long, it seems like a feast to gaze upon lush, fertile ground. I'm sure the horses and cattle look forward to a day off in the welcoming hills; it's not just the weary travelers who yearn for a break.

I've found that I enjoy carrying baby Jenny as often as possible. Cobb seems grateful whenever I volunteer my arms for his baby girl. Having three young children can be challenging enough, but managing a rolling home, a small herd of cattle, and an orchard of thirsty twigs must be all the more difficult.

It would be impossible not to notice that about a quarter of our troupe frowns judgmentally when they see the precious dark-skinned baby in my arms. As long as I live, I'll never understand how anybody can think that the color of somebody's skin makes them more or less human than another. I never expected slavery would still be tolerated in the States. It's bad enough that it couldn't be abolished when our country was founded, but it's 1850 now. There should be no such thing as slavery.

My philosophizing is interrupted by the loud arrival of the friends, Bobby and Wayne. It's unusual for men to visit with other travelers during travel days. More commonly, the womenfolk wander along, in search of conversation.

The triumphant young men are all atwitter. Bobby says, "I'm gonna be a daddy."

Wayne slaps his friend on the back and says, "Me too. And that's not all. My sister's gonna have a baby too." The blond man in the red shirt doubles over laughing.

Bobby says, "Yeah, but I was first. I'll bet Serena's a month or two ahead of Drucilla." It is as if Bobby thinks that makes him more of a man than his brother-in-law.

Wayne seems surprised by Bobby's statement. "But you only found out today, just like me. How do you know how far along they are?"

Bobby shrugs. "Just do."

I try to distract the young men with rowdy congratulations. I pump their hands with my free arm, despite the painful impact on my delicate ribs and the rope burns on my palms. "You must be very proud. Your children will be best friends and double cousins. How exciting. The girls must be delighted."

Bobby says, "Serena's sick as a dog."

Wayne doubles over laughing. "She always had a weak stomach. Drucilla's not sick at all. Why, she practically glows."

I step forward and look more closely at Wayne's face. "What's that on your face," I ask.

Wayne's mood changes. His fingers reach for his chin. "My beard? That what you're talking about? What of it?"

"Oh, I'm sorry. I didn't mean to insult you." Then I look at Bobby. "You also?"

Bobby flashes his eyebrows at me. "We're trying to see who can grow a bushier beard. My whiskers are so long they curl." Bobby pulls his beard and lets go of the ends, then they snap back into place. It might be impressive if it appeared more uniformly across his face. Sometimes, I think men are more fixated on their beards than women are on their hair. I think of Larkin and the many hundreds of hours he spent proudly twisting the ends of his mustache. It seems like years since he died, but it's only been months. So much has happened since then, and yet, I am so far away from realizing the goal we shared.

Jenny gurgles and I'm brought back to the present. I quickly tell Bobby and Wayne that both of them are well on the way. "We'll have to wait until the end of our journey to decide which beard is most impressive." Hopefully, that will prevent the best friends from baring their fists at each other until then. "But if you want to make the wagon ladies jealous of your wives, you'll sharpen your razors and scrape those beards off."

Wayne says, "Don't you like beards, Mrs. Moon."

"No, I do not. But, please, call me Dorcas, friend."

Bobby says, "Do all women feel that way?"

I rub my chin. "I've never thought about it, Bobby. Maybe some women prefer kissing thorny shrubs and pricker bushes, but I do not."

Bobby buries his face in his hands, and Wayne's cheeks blaze red. It amuses me to think that they are embarrassed. Bobby says, "Mrs. Moon! Why, that's almost vulgar." His eyes twinkle, and he seems entertained.

I wink at him and say, "You can call me Dorcas also. How about that?"

"Yes, ma'am."

Before the boys make their way to the next wagon, I tell them that they'll make great fathers if only they can refrain from killing each other. That only seems to remind them of what they were fighting about on the day I met them in the streets of Independence. I send them on their way. "Don't make me put a boot to ya. Git along, now. Ya hear?"

As they make their way forward, Bobby says, "I've got a jug of whiskey I've been saving for the Fourth of July. Tomorrow, we are celebrating!"

As I watch the eager future fathers go, I wonder how many others have been saving spirits for the nation's biggest holiday. Then I chuckle at the thought. We're not even in organized territory, let alone the United States.

After we reach Fort Bridger, we spend the afternoon coaxing Gwibunzi into letting a saddle sit on her back. It's too soon to drop a rider in the saddle, but it's a step forward. She's even willing to allow the strap to be tightened around her girth, which reminds me of my abandoned corset. I sure am glad to be rid of that.

Thursday, July 4

Instead of waking to trumpet blasts, the early morning sounds of travelers preparing for a predawn departure jostle me from my dreams. Bellowing cattle, whinnying horses, braying mules, grunting people, and snorts from beasts of every sort fill the air with active noise. The sounds of clumping hooves, jangling chains, and the banging of belongings hooked to wagon sides add to the commotion. When an angry dog starts barking, I shimmy into my clothes and extricate myself from our wagon.

I bring last night's fire back to life. Wood is plentiful to the south of Fort Bridger and having access to it seems like a luxury. When the coffee is ready, I relax as the neighboring wagon trains set their wheels on the trail. First, one string of wagons departs southward along the Mormon Trail, and a short while later, another follows. I wonder why they don't combine their numbers. Perhaps one is bound for the Great Salt Lake and the other heads for California.

Larkin's dream of a safe full of gold comes to mind. I recall how we used to bicker about whether to go to California or Oregon. I shake my head and remember him telling me that perhaps our luck would have been different if we had set out for California. Either way, we would have traveled at least this far, so I don't see how our luck could have been otherwise.

After breakfast, I ask Stillman and the children to help me unload the wagon. If it weren't for my sore body, I would unload it myself. The holiday gives us a chance to rest and relax, but it is also a good time to take stock and prepare. I open each sack and pop the top off every crate. My lip curls when I look into a bag of flour and see mealworms. I would discard the flour, but scarcity might force us to use it despite the infestation. I can sift the mealworms from the meal, and the children can use them to bait their hooks.

Andrew makes a list of needed goods so we will not forget anything. He hands me the list, and I notice the last entry, 'ink.' When the last of our neighbors have departed, we make our way to the fort. A rickety gate tilts outward, welcoming us into the complex, surrounded by a crude fence of pointy-topped posts.

Inside, rough-hewn buildings and log cabins almost remind us of civilization. The rhythmic clang of a blacksmith hammering iron against an anvil fills the air. Three scruffy, bearded men sit outside the trading post, smoking pipes and drinking coffee. The one nearest the door tips his hat and says, "Howdy, ma'am." As we file past him and enter the shop, the men return to their conversation.

Though it is early in the season, there isn't a great variety of trade goods. I'm careful with our remaining funds and limit our purchases to essentials. In addition to flour, beans, bacon, and coffee, I purchase Andrew's ink but cringe at the proprietor's markup. I should be grateful to find *any* indigo, but I wish it weren't ten times what it cost in Independence. The cheerful clerk promises to have a boy deliver our purchases in an hour. When I turn to tell Stillman and the children that it is time to return to camp, everyone is gone. I look back at the clerk, and she says that I can find them outside with her husband, his partner, and their friend.

Beyond the threshold, the children sit on the ground facing the trading post. As I join them, the man beside the door concludes his story about an encounter with a grizzly bear.

Christopher leans forward eagerly. "Then what happened."

The storyteller was ready for the boy's question. "I'll tell you what happened! He ate me, and he spit out my clothes." He pauses, and it's as if he were counting off the seconds to assure his punchline is perfectly timed. "I never was a fancy dresser." The man runs his hands up his suspenders, straps between thumbs and forefingers, then waves at me. "Pardon, folks. Glad you could join us, ma'am. A lady shouldn't have to sit on the ground. One of you scoundrels, get up and offer this lady a seat."

"Thank you, sir, but I'm content to stand. When it comes down to it, I'm more of a lumberjack than a lady anyway."

"Very well, I'm not much of a 'sir' either, now that you mention it. Folks call me Ol' Gabe. This here is my partner, Ol' Vaskiss, and that there is our friend, Lucky Nye."

I gasp. "Did you say, 'Nye?'"

"Yes, do you know each other?"

I shake my head. My mouth opens and my lips move, but words are slow to form. I point at the big man, and say, "I saw you in Spotted Tail's camp."

Lucky Nye is tall, even seated. "Yes, ma'am. That *was* me." He looks at me from the corner of his eye. "Now that you mention it, I remember you also. Imagine the coincidence of seeing you again."

I lean forward a little to look closely at the man, and my hands cover my mouth.

He says, "What's the matter, lady? It looks as though you've seen a ghost."

"I'm sorry, Mr. Nye. It's just... It's just that you remind me of somebody."

Lucky laughs, "As many people as there are in the world, I guess we all look like somebody." Then he reminds me to call him Lucky.

"Yes, Lucky. I'm sure you're right. The only thing is, the man you remind me of is also named Mr. Nye, though he's a little young for the mister part."

Lucky gulps. "You must be mistaken, ma'am. All my children are breeds. Where is *your* Mr. Nye from?"

"Virginia. Or Maryland. Somewhere around those parts of the country."

The man leans forward, rubs his forehead roughly, and pulls his giant hands down his rugged face until his pale blue eyes peek at me from above his fingertips. "How can it be? I... I... what's *this* Mr. Nye's first name. How old is he? Where is he now?"

Ol' Gabe and Ol' Vaskiss chortle at their friend's discomfort, and I can't help laughing as well. When Lucky removes his hat and swings his straight brown hair from his forehead, I'm absolutely certain that what I suspected is true. Lucky's eyes are identical to Alvah's and the way he flips his hair to the side is eerily familiar.

I say, "Mr. Nye, today is your lucky day. You're gonna be a daddy. Your brand-new baby boy is, well, I guess he's about twenty. He's smart, kind, and handsome. He's big as a tree, strong as an ox, and traveling with our wagons to Oregon. Don't try to deny it, sir. Your boy has blue eyes, straight brown hair, and if I ever saw a man that was the spitting image of his father, it's Alvah Nye."

Lucky expels his breath through his lips like the blow of a horse. He says, "You have got to be kidding me, lady. Er. Lumberjack. I mean, ma'am."

Ol' Gabe slaps his thigh, and Ol' Vaskiss looks into the sky and says, "I don't believe it."

Christopher jumps from the ground. "You're Alvah's father? How about that! I'll go get him." I could call after Christopher and try to stop him, but he's gone by the time I fill my lungs with air. His broken arm does nothing to hamper his running speed. I wonder what he plans to tell Alvah.

The stunned mountain man rocks forward and back on his bench. His hands move along his thighs like the runners of a sled on snow. Sweat beads on his forehead, yet he shivers like he's going to freeze to death. Lucky's eyes dart back and forth from me to his friends, then off into the distance.

I try to put the man at ease by telling him about our journey and what a good role model Alvah is for my son, Christopher. The more I talk, the tenser he becomes. It looks like the poor man is about to burst into flames or explode like a keg of gunpowder.

Lucky drags his forearm across his brow again, glances sideways at me, and takes a deep breath. He raises his eyebrows and says, "It's a lot to take in, Mrs... Um, er. What is your name again, ma'am?"

"Oh, dear. Please forgive my manners. I told you, I'm not much of a lady. I am Dorcas Moon, and these are my children, Stillman, Rose, Andrew, and Dahlia Jane." Stillman's eyes grow wide. This is the first time I've introduced Stillman in this manner. "The boy that ran off is my son, Christopher."

The tense mountain man begins to squirm. "And you just... met... Alvah... when you joined the same wagon train?" The way he says Alvah makes the big man seem as vulnerable as a newborn fawn.

I answer. "That's right. But Alvah's become like a member of our family." I glance at Stillman, then back at the fidgety trapper.

When Christopher drags Alvah through the open gate, Mr. Nye stands. The muscles in the older man's face sag, and his mouth hangs open as the younger man who looks just like him draws nearer.

Alvah plants his feet in the dirt just inside the fort's walls. Honey sits, heeling, beside his left leg. Christopher's efforts to drag Alvah closer fail to budge his mountainous mentor.

Lucky stands facing Alvah, and the two men look like gunfighters meeting each other on the streets of a turbulent town at noon rather than kin. I'm reminded of the gunfighters that dueled in Independence.

It's a temptation to take Lucky's hand and pull him toward Alvah. Instead, I place my left hand on Lucky's nearest shoulder and reach my right arm across the rugged explorer's muscular back. He flinches when I touch him. I say, "Everything will be fine, Lucky. You'll see."

Mr. Nye takes small steps, like a man making a slow walk toward the gallows. If I were him, I think I would run as fast as I could toward the son

I never had, throw my arms around him, and smother him with a lifetime of hugs and kisses.

Alvah's legs begin to move, and he takes a tentative step forward. His obedient, four-legged companion matches his forward progress. Alvah is close enough that I can see the expression on his face.

Father and son approach one another like turtles. It crosses my mind that two decades separate these men. That's a lot of ground to cover in a few short steps.

Finally, I stand before Alvah with my arms around the father that he thought was dead. I say, "Alvah. I'd like you to meet this man whose friends call him Lucky." The thin mountain air feels thick as axle grease as I continue my introduction. "Lucky, this is Alvah Nye, a good and strong man that anyone would be proud to call son."

The father extends his hand. I look down and watch their hands clasp in greeting. Their oversized paws look like perfect duplicates. I've heard of identical twins but never met any. Looking at Alvah and Lucky almost feels like looking at the same person, now and in the future. As I look up from their handshake, I think that the son may be an inch taller.

I try to break the tension by speaking to Alvah. "Come and meet Lucky's friends."

Lucky and Alvah release their grip and turn toward the trading post. Ol' Gabe stands from his chair and reaches for his partner's elbow. Instead of using nicknames, the man says, "I'm Jim Bridger, and this is my partner, Luis Vázquez."

My eyes blink in stunned surprise. Somehow, I had missed the fact that Ol' Gabe was the notorious mountain man and proprietor of the Fort that bears his name.

Alvah looks at one legendary mountain man, and then the other, and introduces himself. Ol' Gabe says, "I reckon you and Lucky got some catching up to do. We'll leave you to it." He extends his arm toward the vacant chairs in front of the trading post and says, "Make yourselves at home."

I'd love to stay and watch, but Alvah and his newfound father need their privacy. Christopher begs to stay with Alvah and Lucky. I hate to disappoint him, but I don't expect the conversation between Alvah and his father is something the boy should infringe upon. I suggest, "Perhaps you can spend time with them later, dear."

He scowls at me. I'm not sure whether it was because I told him no or because I called him *dear*.

During the day, three other wagon trains arrive at Fort Bridger. The remote outpost feels like a crowded city. In addition to the emigrants and residents, there must be a hundred teepees near the woods to the southwest of the fort.

Everyone dresses in their finest clothes and parades around the fort's perimeter at four. Those who have instruments do their best to play together as a marching band. The unrehearsed music is festive despite the hodgepodge. Garland Knox proudly carries a red, white, and blue flag on a stick.

After the parade, everyone gathers outside the fort's walls for a picnic. Ol' Gabe generously provides an elk. Lucky and Ol' Vaskiss help him roast the meat over a central fire. Everybody brings something to contribute to the feast. Many of us had no choice but to cook the usual fare, but something about eating somebody else's cooking makes for a memorable occasion. The musicians continue playing, taking turns wolfing down their suppers.

Some men and perhaps a couple of the ladies have been drinking. I've been watching Galusha and Samuel from the corner of my eye, and I've noticed that Samuel's wife, Edna, takes a nip when the men are distracted.

As they planned, Bobby and Wayne have also been drinking. Nearby, Bobby Bond slaps his buddy's back and says, "I bet you can't ride Dorcas' mustang."

Wayne says, "I reckon I can if you can."

"I'll bet you a dollar I can stay on twice as long as you can."

"You're on. That is if you can talk *the widow* into letting us try."

How dare they? I'm about to object to being referred to as *the widow* when Ol' Gabe taps my shoulder. He says, "Excuse me, Dorcas, ma'am. Did these boys say you have a mustang?"

I turn to him and say, "Why, yes—goodness gracious. I roped the wild mare in a canyon last week. She hasn't been ridden yet. Would you like to see her?"

Our host says, "Maybe we could help you break the bronco. I'll put up a prize for the first man who can ride the horse." He smiles and says, "It might prevent a fight, ma'am. There's nothing like a wild horse to take the edge off when men get to drinking."

Despite my better judgment, I consent. I'm worried that one of our celebrants will mistreat the horse, and she'll never be the same afterward. Somehow, I'm not inclined to deny our famous host's request.

Ol' Gabe introduces me to his wife. Then he says, "Little Fawn is chief Washakie's daughter."

I tell the woman that it is a pleasure to make her acquaintance and then ask if Crimson Dawn is her mother. Ol' Gabe looks at me with a tilted head. "How do you know Washakie's wife?" I tell him that I met Little Fawn's parents at the Birthing Stone before finding the mustang.

The mountain man says, "Well, I'll be...." and his voice trails off. Then he says, "Let's clear off a table, and I'll make an announcement."

Bobby and Wayne try to interrupt, and I hold a finger up. "Just a minute, boys. Our host has an announcement to make. You might want to get ready to be first in line." They look at each other, each mirroring the other's surprised expression. They look to me like quarrelsome school children rather than expectant fathers.

Ol' Gabe asks me how quickly we can get the horse. I suggest perhaps fifteen minutes. He asks who the fastest runner is. I spy Dembi Koofai leaning against the palisade walls and wave him over. He's slow to understand that I am signaling him, but runs to me when he realizes I'm waving at him. I ask, "Would you get Gwibunzi for me?"

The mountain man asks, "Do you speak Shoshone? I thought you said that you were from New York."

I smile at the man. "The scout, Dembi Koofai, has taught me a few Shoshone words, and his friend has taught me some hand signs." I glance at the scout's chest. The scorpion's body is gone. A single pincer remains, delicately clinging to the Shoshone's dark brown skin.

Ol' Gabe says, "Well, how about that?" He scratches his chin, parting the whiskers of his beard. "Don't that beat all?"

The limber mountaineer leaps onto the table and announces a wild horse riding competition. He offers a cash prize of $5 for the first rider who can stay on for more than five minutes and tells everyone who is interested to line up behind me.

Bobby and Wayne leap forward, pushing and shoving each other aside. It isn't long before fists are flying. I look at Ol' Gabe, wondering if he plans to say anything or intervene.

The best friends wrestle each other to the ground. Blue arms twine with red, and a roaring crowd quickly closes in. If there's something people like watching as much as a horse riding competition, it's a fist fight. When the worst enemies break away and find their feet, I snatch the back of Wayne's shirt and pull him toward me. Bobby crashes to the ground where his best friend stood a half-second earlier.

I say to Wayne, "Bobby will go first, and you will go second."

When Bobby stands again, he plants his feet and prepares to swing at Wayne. I tell him that he may go first and that his brother-in-law will wait his turn. Then, I whisper to Wayne that going second will give him better odds. What does it matter anyway? Neither young man has a chance, but perhaps Ol' Gabe is right. A bucking horse is just what our nation's 74th birthday needs. Never mind that we're celebrating on Mexican soil, rather than within the United States' territory. Then again, now that the war with Mexico is over, it's hard to surmise what government has jurisdiction over the land beneath Jim Bridger and Luis Vázquez's fort.

The fracas has perfectly filled the time Dembi Koofai needed to return with Gwibunzi. It has also warmed up the crowd. The contestants quickly separate from the spectators. An assortment of mountain men, settlers, and Indians has lined up, preparing to take a chance at winning five dollars. Who knows how many side bets have been placed, as well.

Gwibunzi's light brown eyelashes and curved neck give her a slightly menacing appearance. Otherwise, the lanky horse looks docile. When the mountain man ties a rope around the horse, her ears pitch back, and her eyes go wild. Her white, third eyelid contrasts brilliantly with her dark eyes and make her look dangerous.

Ol' Vaskiss cups his hands together and boosts Bobby onto Gwibunzi's back. Ol' Gabe hands the lead rope to the young man, and the mustang takes off. She bucks high, lifting her front legs skyward. Her body corkscrews, quickly pitching Bobby into the air. Before he hits the ground, Lucky Nye reaches his arms forward and catches Bobby Bond in his arms. With a chuckle, the mountain man sets the disoriented rapscallion on the ground.

It takes a few minutes to get ahold of the lead rope and bring the mustang back into position. Wayne licks his lips and hoists his tight trousers before nodding to Ol' Vaskiss. Wayne Horton lasts seconds longer than his brother-in-law.

The wild mare efficiently pitches every rider to dirt. The last contestant is my mild-mannered friend, Charlie O. Banyon. I wish Cobb good luck, and he flashes the bright smile that always reminds me to be strong during times of adversity.

Before Cobb mounts Gwibunzi, he caresses the tired horse's muzzle, whispers soothing words in a low voice, and strokes her sweaty neck. It is as if he were reminding the horse of their special friendship.

The mustang makes a good show of trying to buck off her last rider. The man who dreams of owning an apple orchard clings to her back like glue. Whether she twists to the left or right, Cobb anticipates her moves like he can read her mind. Just when the bronco seems spent, somebody throws firecrackers at her feet.

The wild horse spins like a demon occupies her soul. Then she takes off at a gallop into the gathered crowd knocking Captain Meadows to the ground. Moments later, Gwibunzi crashes with a grunt into the fort's outer wall, which wobbles but holds. The horse turns back toward the crowd, breathing hard, and stands still. She turns her head in one direction and then another. If I could read Gwibunzi's mind, I imagine that today's riders haven't fully convinced her that she wants to be domesticated.

Ol' Gabe says, "This man still has another minute left to go. Anyone object to proclaiming him the winner now?"

I glance to the side and see Samuel Grosvenor strike a friction match. Galusha Gains leans over a handful of firecrackers. I should have figured that the delinquents were not juveniles. My feet move before I realize that I'm headed for a confrontation. Galusha doesn't see me coming. When I tackle the scoundrel, he lands on his back as the firecrackers in his hand explode on his chest. The lout smells like he bathed in whiskey. When the shock of our collision registers, Galusha curses Cobb, stringing together stinging racial epithets.

I struggle to find my feet, and Galusha tries to stand as well. Despite my sore body and aching muscles, I grit my teeth and find the strength to push him back to the ground with my foot. Turning to the crowd, I say, "Instead of doing what's right, why do men stand by?"

The grumbling crowd shrinks away from me. Men tilt their heads forward, hiding their eyes beneath hat brims. Ol' Gabe says, "Looks like you've got the matter taken care of, Marshal Moon." Then he shakes Cobb's hand.

Bobby congratulates Cobb. The black cowboy winks at Bobby and says, "Sometimes it pays to be the last in line."

FRIDAY, JULY 5

FOR THOSE WHO CELEBRATED late and drank too much, our extended stay at Fort Bridger allows for sleeping late. Most travelers sleep in, but those of us who are such creatures of habit that we can't slumber past dawn do our best to start the day quietly.

At eight, Agapito and Arikta pass slowly through camp. "It would be a good day to cut grass, *estimada*. There is not much ahead of us." We're directed to a bountiful meadow and spend most of the day gathering sheaves and swimming in the Blacks Fork River.

When we return to camp, late in the afternoon, we find a stranger by our fire. A short man with a wild face jumps to his feet and greets us like long-lost relatives. His arm pulls back and forth like a misery whip. That's what lumberjacks call a two-man saw. The jolly man introduces himself. "George Traverse, at your service, ma'am." He winks at me and says, "Most folks just call me Muddy George."

As the man introduces himself to Stillman and the children, I wonder how he got his nickname. It could be the man's wild hair, long thick beard, and expressive eyebrows are the reason for the moniker. Though he looks old enough to have gone gray, his hair is a dead match for the dirt-colored rivers, somewhere between dirty blond and sandy brown. Muddy George's wide-set eyes stand above the flared nostrils of his nose, and his cavernous mouth looks like he's hoping for a big meal of mosquitoes. When he returns his attention to me, he gestures toward his nearby cart. "Would you like to inspect my wares, Miss Dorcas? Step on up and take a look-see. Maybe you can help a tired old coot lighten his load." While he speaks, his fat grin never diminishes.

It doesn't seem possible to tell the man no. How much money do we need to save for passage, tolls, and ferries ahead? The less money we have, the more carefully it must be hoarded, but something about the peddler makes me curious. What could it hurt to see what the man has in his strange, half-sized wagon? Stillman and the children follow me to Muddy George's cart.

As we approach, his team sounds off. A man whose livelihood depends on attracting customers should not employ animals who make such offensive sounds. I'm not sure whether the four mismatched donkeys are hungry, thirsty, or bored. I ask Muddy George if I can bring the braying beasts a pail of water.

"Naw, I just brought them back from the river. They just like to hear the sound of their own voices." It's hard to talk with the see-sawing sound of braying donkeys close by.

Boss Wheel ambles over from next door. Muddy George greets him like a best friend or favorite cousin. "Boss Wheel! Good to see you, Mr. Roulette. You look good, *mon ami*."

Not one to engage in small talk, Boss Wheel graciously shakes the peddler's hand. "Got any of them flavored toothpicks left?"

"Most certainly do. My specialty, don't you know. If memory serves, you cotton to the pickle-flavored ones, isn't that right, Boss?"

Our surly leader looks at me as he says to the man, "Keeps unwanted visitors away. Whatta you get for 'em these days?"

Muddy George names his price. Boss Wheel grunts his dissatisfaction at the traveling salesman and produces a coin from a waistcoat pocket. As fast as the ramrod appeared, he's gone. The peddler returns his attention to the kids and me.

My fingers seem to have found a mane comb. Muddy George looks at my hair and then back at the mane comb and I know what he's thinking. Being as good a salesman as he is, I'm sure he will not make the mistake of suggesting that the comb will work as well on people as it does on horses. Wisely, he says, "Would you like to see some ribbons and bows, Miss Dorcas?" He looks at Rose and Dahlia Jane, and says, "Maybe the pretty flowers would like something nice to go in their hair." He hands me a delicate hand mirror. "Maybe the girls would like one of these."

"We have a mirror, Muddy George. Thank you just the same."

His wild eyes cast about. "Maybe you want some tea. How about a table-cloth? Got enough needles and thread? A magnifying glass? I got some of those new-fangled safety pins. I have a couple of bolts of fabric." George glances at Stillman. "I got tobaccy." Stillman shakes his head and the man looks at Christopher and then Andrew. "A compass? Pocket knife? Tom-myhawk? Lead pencils?"

I wander to the other side of the cart. Muddy George holds a bright green ribbon beside Dahlia Jane's head and makes a suggestive grunt. I see his lamps and ask about matches. He jumps forward and produces matches and reminds me that toothpicks are his specialty.

"Are they all pickle-flavored?"

He holds his belly and laughs. As his guffaw winds down, his laughter sounds like the donkeys. I wonder whether he follows their example or if it is the other way around. "Naw, Miss Dorcas. I have cinnamon, mint, lemon, and cedar-flavored toothpicks. Made 'em myself. Which would you like to have?"

I poll the children and they can't agree. Muddy George suggests, "A package of each then, Miss Dorcas?"

The merchant talks me into a measure of green ribbon for Dahlia Jane, a package of toothpicks for each of the children and for Stillman, and I can't resist the mane comb, despite our depleted treasury.

I should have asked how much it would cost before agreeing to purchase these items. When he answers the question, "How much?" I set everything back down and start to walk away. When he dickers himself down from two dollars to one dollar, I consent to the transaction, hand George the dollar, and apologize. "We haven't got all that much money left. We need to save everything we can. Are you sure that a dollar is enough?"

He laughs. "I reckon so, Miss Dorcas. I always start high. Never know what I might get away with, you see. Don't cost much to make toothpicks, but it takes a lot of work to drag all this stuff up and down the trails, you see."

The kindly peddler wishes everyone a good evening. Somehow, he remembers everybody's name.

SATURDAY, JULY 6

WE TURN OUR BACKS to the vibrant Uinta Mountains and head north by northwest. The barren terrain quickly dominates our journey. It was nice to have a holiday from it, but we've grown accustomed to the arid landscape. We leave Fort Bridger with two additional passengers. Lucky Nye plans to tag along until we reach the Raft River. Muddy George doesn't say how long he plans to accompany us.

The traveling salesman agrees to be interviewed for *The Rolling Home Times*, and Andrew is excited to feature the well-traveled man. I don't believe the peddler intends to panic us, but when I hear him answer Andrew's questions about the dangers ahead, I can't help being frightened myself. Evidently, the outlaws that killed Landon Young and Grace Weaver's brother-in-law last summer have *not* retired, as Leon Humphries suggested. Their legend has grown. Muddy George claims that at least a dozen emigrants have been killed by the bandits. Many travelers complain that Indians steal their horses and cattle, but Muddy George believes that it's really the outlaws who are responsible for the stolen stock. Andrew asks whether it's just one group of pirates or many. Muddy George isn't sure

of the answer but suggests that the army should pay attention to the trail
rather than just buying and building fortresses along the way.

I rub my temples as we walk along. What will happen when Andrew posts
his interview at The Hub tonight? If the past is any indication, Boss Wheel
is not going to like it one bit. But, as Andrew said when he posted the letter
Sarah Terwilliger sent to her brother, the emigrants have a right to know
the dangers they'll face.

When Andrew forgets to stake *The Times* upon arrival at Muddy Creek,
I'm relieved. Our refreshed Devons kept a good pace today, and we have
much of the afternoon to ourselves. I retreat to the cover of the wagon
and change my dress. My bruises have turned from black and blue to a
sickly yellow, but they feel less tender to the touch. I wonder whether I
should ask Dr. Appleyard to take a look at them. I have no choice but to
put my tattered dress back on. Who cares? Not me. My legs are covered.
I'm sure that Dottie Crouse would not approve, but what difference does it
make? Absent-mindedly, I pull the mane comb from the pocket of Larkin's
trousers and rake it through my thick hair. By the time I realize what I'm
doing, I'm finished. Maybe it would horrify another woman to brush her
hair with a horse's comb, but not me. I can't help but chuckle as I depart
the wagon.

I spend the rest of the afternoon dragging the metal comb through Gwibunzi's mane and tail. I'm surprised that the wild mare allows me to groom
her. It isn't easy to remove a lifetime of snarls all at once. I should be
scrubbing clothes against the washboard instead of brushing a horse's hair,
but how clean could I get the clothes with water that comes from an
estuary named Muddy Creek?

As I comb Gwibunzi's tail, I think of all of the devastation caused by the pirates ahead. How will I keep my friends and family safe? We've lost enough people already. What if rustlers steal our oxen? How will we get to Oregon if we don't have our cattle to pull the wagon? What will I do if they steal our horses? It would break my heart to lose any of our animals now. I've always loved Blizzard, and yet I couldn't stand to lose Gwibunzi either. I've grown to love old Hardtack too. I realize that my fear of wolves has given way to being petrified of what the outlaws will do, and then, like Dahlia Jane fantasizes about people with cat faces, I see a pack of snarling pirates with dog faces and patches over wolfish eyes. Is the long daily trudge responsible for such outlandish notions?

The mane comb is full of tangled horsehair. Though her coat is mottled, her tail is solid brown, and it reminds me of the color of Muddy George's long hair and beard. The powerful mustang looks much more civilized to me now. Will Captain Meadows accept her now that she looks so refined?

While pulling clumps of hair from the comb and releasing them into a swift breeze, I hear the long wail of a bow across fiddle strings. Then, a banjo joins in. Where did that come from? I didn't know that we had a banjo player among us. It's Saturday night, but I hadn't expected a dance so soon after celebrating the Fourth of July.

I wash my hands in Muddy Creek, put the mane comb in my pocket, and notice that another wagon train has arrived. Somehow, I missed their appearance while daydreaming and grooming my horse.

I make my way to The Hub just as Andrew knocks the top of the post with a rock. I take a deep breath and look around at the crowd. The travelers from the other wagon train have been drawn to our circle by the inviting sound of music. Hopefully, square dancing and darkening skies will distract people from the news of the day.

I turn toward the musicians, and I'm surprised to see Muddy George playing the banjo. As animated as the peddler gets when he meets people, it is nothing compared to the exuberance on display when he picks the banjo strings. I look at Agapito and his eyes lock with mine. I walk forward until I can see the dimples at the corner of his mouth, and know that his warm smile is directed at me.

If only fantasy could become reality. What if dreams could come true? Instead of feeling optimistic, I'm consumed with worry about the dangers that lie ahead. We should have stayed at Fort Bridger and built a small cabin along Blacks Fork River.

I could get rich selling scones to travelers instead of getting robbed by highwaymen after traveling thousands of miles from home.

SUNDAY, JULY 7

IN THE MORNING, OUR fellow travelers lift anchor, uncoil their circled wagons, and ride north along the trail that we will follow tomorrow. As I heat coffee in the blue speckled pot, Muddy George's donkeys bray. Evidently, the peddler is departing with the other wagon train. Of all the places to spend an extra day, so far this is the worst.

My fingertips run across the teeth of the comb through the fabric of my trousers. It was an extravagant purchase and a luxury I could have done without. Gwibunzi's mane and tail could eventually have been straightened with my fingers or a forked stick, but I'm glad I spent the money on the trader's toothpicks and the mane comb.

A blood-curdling scream disrupts my thoughts. I look up from the fire toward The Hub and see Addie Bull. She drops the wooden flap over the published newspaper, and her hands find her face. She turns and runs toward her wagon, no doubt in a hurry to tell Pious what she read.

I look to the heavens when I see Horace Blocker trot toward the post, and can't help stepping in that direction myself. Horace Blocker never runs anywhere. There's no putting off what I know is coming. I stand a short distance away as Horace lowers the flap and looks at me. His lips form a giant circle in the middle of his face. Then he closes his mouth and says, "We're doomed. Nobody is going to make it to Oregon, are they? We're goners, every last one of us."

Though he asked me a question, I'm sure he didn't mean for me to answer. Nevertheless, I say to the man, "Nobody should have to worry about being killed or robbed along the trail. It's a terrible thing to hear about so many crimes. I know it sounds dangerous, Horace, but that doesn't mean that *everyone* will be killed. We must be vigilant. We must learn how to defend ourselves. We must do everything we can to help our guides keep us safe. What else can we do?"

The petrified man says, "I don't care if it is Sunday morning. I need a drink." I cross my arms and watch the naysayer scamper back to his wagon. What good will getting drunk do? Wouldn't it be better to prepare our defenses?

Galusha and Samuel appear beside me with a grunt, startling me, and I listen as the hunter reads the news to his sidekick, who I suspect cannot read. I look at Galusha's hunched back, but in my mind, I can see his lip curl as he reads Andrew's interview of Muddy George. When Galusha finishes, he turns to me and says, "Don't worry, missy. I'm ready for a fight. I'll protect you, your addle-brained girlie, and your whole sorry family. It's time a hunter was in charge of this wagon train instead of a preacher."

I should know better than to try to talk to Galusha, but can't help myself. "That's what the wagon master and his crew are for. They're here to protect us from dangers like this. That's why we signed on with experienced guides who've been to Oregon several times."

Galusha frowns at me and reminds me that Sarah Terwilliger's husband traveled with Boss Wheel last year. Samuel echoes Galusha's words, "Yeah. Don't forget about that fact. Remember Sarah. Poor, Sarah Terwilliger." Usually, Samuel just says a word or two rather than utter a complete sentence. To listen to the man, one would think he was personally acquainted with the brave widow.

I was right to worry about Andrew's newspaper. As the word spreads, people mill about in the middle of the wagon train. I walk to the master's camp and tell Agapito about Andrew's interview. He makes a face, and I know he dreads having to inform Boss Wheel. "I must tell him, no? I am sorry, *estimada*. He would not forgive me if I did not. You know that he does not like surprises."

I watch as the assistant wagon master saddles Rio and rides a short distance to the north of camp. Fifteen minutes later, Clipper gallops into camp, and Boss Wheel dismounts. I can hear his angry boots stomp from his wagon to The Hub. I watch from my wagon and imagine smoke billowing from his ears as he slowly reads *The Times*.

As he turns toward me, I hold my breath. His stomping feet make their way along the imaginary spoke that leads from The Hub to my wagon. The closer he gets, the more ready I am to face him. It's not my fault that Sarah Terwilliger's husband was killed last year. Nor is it because of me that outlaws lie in wait to murder, rob, and maim us, if that is indeed what they plan to do. I didn't ask Muddy George to incite a riot, but I'm proud of Andrew, and I'm glad he's warned everybody about what to expect.

I cross my arms again as Boss Wheel takes his final steps. Instead of making a rational argument, the man simply says, "I should have never let you sign up with us. I knew you were trouble the moment I laid eyes on you."

The man turns away from me so quickly it takes a moment for his long arms to swing around in place as he makes his exit. He spits on the ground beside him and rages forward to his trusty steed. The mountain man swings a leg over Clipper's rump and lopes back up the trail to the north of camp.

Meanwhile, I fume. It is as if the dunderheaded fool blames me instead of the outlaws, the trail, or himself. For a fraction of a second, I wonder if we might be better off having Galusha Gains lead us the rest of the way to Oregon. Good Heavens, what a dreadful thought to think. What a dreadful trip that would make. I take a deep breath and exhale. I understand Boss Wheel's blustering nature. He's kind of like Larkin, only twice as disagreeable.

I should take it as a compliment that the grizzly loner is comfortable confronting me. He barely speaks to anyone else, except for Agapito.

Monday, July 8

It's WELL AFTER DARK following an arduous travel day. The air is thin, yet it feels heavy. There's a new moon, and it is a dark night.

I have watch duty with Lucky and Alvah. The father and son sit near the picketed horses, and I march the dark perimeter of the encampment, singing as I go.

Agapito says that cattle like to hear a comforting voice; it helps mollify them. Someone should sing to the traveling masses as we march the days away. If it would placate their worries, I would do it myself. I imagine riding Blizzard back and forth along the line, cooing lullabies at my fellow emigrants, and chuckle to myself.

A strange sound catches my ear and stops my feet. I've just completed a lap around the oxen, and I'm near the horses at the picket line. Lucky and Alvah are ten feet away from me. Abruptly, they stand and peer toward the creek into the darkness. The noise must have also attracted their attention.

At first, it sounds like the kind of noises cattle make, but after a couple of seconds, the low growling becomes deeper and louder. I also hear water splashing. I clutch Larkin's rifle and prepare myself to fire it. After a few quick steps, I reach my fellow guards and whisper, "What is it?"

Even in the darkness, I can tell that Lucky is uncomfortable. Without looking at me, he says, "There's a bear out there. I can always tell when a grizzly is near. I do hate 'em. Shore do."

I ask, "What should we do?"

Lucky says, "Usually, I'd back away and hope the bruin has other plans."

Our brief conversation is interrupted by a commotion among the cattle. The bellowing cows sound agitated, and the little herd begins to run. The horses' feet stomp nervously, and they tug at the picket line. Between growls, the bear grunts, and then there is a dragging sound.

Alvah cocks his rifle and speaks between his teeth. "Gotta get closer."

Lucky looks like he just wants to get farther away. "If it weren't for the pilgrims, we should go the opposite way."

I gulp. We must protect our sleeping companions. We tiptoe through the darkness toward the scary sounds. There's one able hunter on either side of me, and three rifles point toward the ominous sound of cracking bones.

At the creek's edge, the enormous bear's claws rip through a yearling calf, then it opens its mouth and tears raw meat from the carcass. Dark as the night is, the fact that we can see what's happening means that we're too close to the bear.

First, Alvah positions his rifle to take a shot, and then, Lucky lifts his gun into position. I follow suit, and Alvah whispers. "Aim for his heart. On three." Then he slowly counts down.

I don't know if all three shots hit the bear, but there's still life in him. The massive beast knows where we are, and he barrels toward us without hesitation.

My hand reaches for the Colt Walker as Alvah says, "Draw your revolvers." But, there's barely time. The behemoth is upon us. I don't remember firing the handgun or whether the hunters got lead into it.

The angry monster crashes between Alvah and me. I feel my body twisting away, and a claw slices through the left leg of Larkin's trousers. As I land in a heap on the ground, I hear the low reverberation of a ferocious roar. Our bullets haven't stopped the devil beast. Instead, it is headed directly toward the wagons.

I don't know what became of Larkin's rifle, but somehow I've managed to keep the revolver in hand. I scramble to my feet without checking myself for injuries. There's no time for that. I run toward the wagons, trying to catch up with Lucky and Alvah. The younger man must have managed to avoid the creature's long arm and sharp claws.

The weary travelers have awakened, and their screams fill the midnight air. Most have remained in their wagons. When I reach the perimeter of the circled wagons, I see the grizzly near The Hub. He stops and stands erect. At the peak of his height, he roars so loudly that the ground shakes. Then, he thunders across the circle away from us.

Alvah says, "Don't shoot. Our bullets might hit people. We can't risk it."

The beast pushes a wagon with his giant paws, crashing the prairie schooner onto its side. Then, the bruin climbs over the wagon box, slicing with his claws, ripping the wagon cover, and collapses within the wreckage.

I lower the Colt Walker and notice the people's screams are louder than before the bear's death. As we make our way toward the fallen beast and the broken wagon, I wonder whose it is.

Frightened women and children run toward The Hub.

Boss Wheel, Agapito, and Arkita arrive beside the tipped wagon at the same time we do. There's movement beneath the shredded wagon bonnet, and a man's loud voice fills the air as his head pokes up. "Can't a fella get a good night's sleep around here? I guess it's my turn to stand watch." He makes a show of yawning and stretching, looks down at the enormous bear, and says, "Look who came a calling." Schuyler flicks a couple of angry bees away

My body relaxes. Thank heavens the bear attacked a single man's wagon rather than one belonging to a family man. Schuyler Steele's good nature helps calm the terrified travelers. It takes ten men to drag the inert carnivore from camp. I watch as Agapito and Arikta butcher the bear, and the rest of the men heave Schuyler's wagon upright. Angry bees drill into them, and they mutter their protests and scamper away as quickly as they can. Then, I make my way to my own wagon. I hope the wild silvertip didn't destroy Schuyler's wagon. The bonnet is undoubtedly ruined, and somebody lost a calf beside the river, but we are fortunate. I was so afraid that the bear would kill someone.

It takes a long time to settle the children. I rock Dahlia Jane in my arms and sing the same song to her that I sang to the cattle while I was on watch. Hours later, when she finally falls asleep, I pray our guides will not awaken us too early.

TUESDAY, JULY 9

DAHLIA JANE AND I are the last ones to wake up in the morning. When I climb from the back of the wagon, the children have completed our morning chores and are ready to travel.

I walk with a bowl of porridge to Schuyler's wagon. The man is lucky. It looks like his wagon is ready to roll, and he has organized his remaining belongings neatly within it. He reassures me that he will be alright. "I can fix the broken rib. All I need is a new cover. Good thing the wagon master carries a spare. Somehow, the hive was unharmed."

I tell the young wheelwright that I'm glad and walk to the bloodstained dirt beyond his wagon. The dead bear's bones and offal lie in a hideous heap beside the gory earth. I try to feel bad about the murderous bruin's demise, but such compassion doesn't find me.

My feet walk along Little Muddy Creek. It is hard to tell the difference between this tributary and the larger Muddy Creek where we camped Saturday and Sunday. Maybe they're different estuaries. It's hard to tell. I guess it doesn't make a difference anyway. The land we're traveling through seems the same from one day to the next, and we should consider ourselves lucky to have access to any water within this desert trek. It's a wonder that whoever blazed this trail was able to find a pathway with sufficient water to sustain such a pilgrimage.

Someone has rounded up the dispersed cattle and gathered them near the river. I look upon the remains of the ox slaughtered by the grizzly. Then something catches my eye in the river, and I step nearer to get a closer look. A half-submerged, weathered wagon lies on its side in the muddy brown water like a shipwreck. I wonder whether that wagon suffered the same fate as Schuyler Steele's. Perhaps this destructive bruin has a history of knocking over wagons and devouring the food within them.

When I return to the wagon, I retrieve Larkin's ripped trousers and fetch the sewing supplies. I have trouble enough with needles and threads without having to punch the sharp tip through thick fabric while walking.

Beneath the abrasive cloth of Larkin's other trousers, the long scabby scar on my leg throbs and itches.

In the peak of summer's heat, the outlaw brothers ride to their favorite lookout spot, a perfect place to survey the trail. They hadn't expected to see anyone and they are surprised to see a man on foot leading a mule along the wrong side of the Snake.

The Viper says, "What do you make of that?" He never expects his brothers to weigh in when he asks himself questions.

Sloan grunts.

The Radish says, "Way he's traveling, he looks like a miner to me." The Radish almost sounds jealous.

The outlaws watch as the man leads his mule up a tributary on the west side of the Snake. The Viper peers through a spyglass and says, "He's headed up Hog Creek. Suppose he's got himself a mine up there?"

The Radish's enthusiasm gushes forth. "Hope so. That'd prove there's gold in these mountains. Maybe I'm not the only one crazy enough to believe in the possibilities." His voice drops off slightly, "Only, I would swear to my mountain, not those one's up there."

The Viper says, "Let's follow. If we don't catch a gold mine, at least we'll get us a mule." He scans the landscape once more and says, "There ain't another soul within miles of here."

The outlaws don't need to hurry to catch up with the old fellow quickly. They descend upon their prey as if he were a minor chore.

The miner turns to greet the approaching brothers. He grins as if glad to have company. "Howdy, friends. Name's Henry. Henry Trudgeon, and this here is Flossie."

The mule curls its lips and bares her teeth as if she were trained to smile during introductions.

"Flossie claims she can smell gold, but I'm not so sure." Unbothered by the lack of a reciprocal introduction, Henry says, "You found any?" It is as if the man were asking another angler whether the fish are biting.

The Radish shifts his weight in the saddle.

Sloan lowers his hat so that it covers more of his head.

Finally, The Viper says, "Not a speck. Where you headed, stranger?"

"Up Hog Creek. I'm working a cave on the east side of Dead Indian Mountain that Flossie thinks looks promising. So far, we ain't found nothing."

The Viper says, "Lead the way."

"You looking for a place to camp for the night? We'd love to have the company." Henry turns toward his mule on the pretense of asking for her consent. "Wouldn't we, Flossie?"

On the way up Hog Creek, Henry chatters a mile a minute. The Viper wonders whether the old miner comprehends the pickle he's in. Sometimes, The Viper has noticed, victims think that they can befriend their captors and talk their way out of a tough spot.

Henry says, "Hey, fellas, would you want to throw in with me? I bet we can find gold faster if we work together. For all I care, you can have most of it. I never wanted to be rich anyhow, I just like discovering things that ain't never been found before."

The Radish squints and looks at his oldest brother.

Sloan yawns.

The Viper's cold blue stare drills into the miner's forehead. "Generous offer. You show us around and we'll let you know if we accept."

When they reach Henry's mine, The Viper is impressed. "How many years you been digging into the side of this mountain?"

Henry leads the brothers through the entrance, talking as he goes. "This will be my fifth summer. The cave was already here. I dug it out some." There's not enough light coming from the mouth of the mine to see its outer edges. There's plenty of room above them, and the cave is spacious enough that three times as many people could fit inside.

"And you ain't found nothing."

"Not yet, but my luck is going to change this year. I just know it."

The Viper begins to speak in a voice familiar to his brothers. It is time to go to work. "Yes, sir old-timer, I agree with you... your luck is going to change this year."

Sloan and The Radish close in on the miner, tightly gripping his elbows.

"Take Mr. Trudgeon back outside, men."

While his brothers hold the miner still, The Viper goes through the old man's saddlebags and unpacks the mule's cargo baskets. The chatty miner continues to try and befriend The Viper and his brothers, answering questions about his possessions as if it were commonplace for a man's belongings to be shared with strangers.

Finally, The Viper says, "Where you want to be planted?"

Henry clears his throat. "What did you say, friend?"

"You heard me."

"You don't have to be like that. Take what you want. I'm glad to help a friend in need, so it ain't even stealing."

"That's not how it's gonna be. If you don't put up a fuss, we'll plant you in the ground rather than feed you to the buzzards. It won't be me does the shoveling, mind you."

The miner sputters. "You can't kill me, friend. My woman will never forgive me if I don't come home. She'll haunt me in the hereafter, something fierce."

Henry's eyes grow wide as The Viper takes the miner's pickaxe from Flossie's back. His eyes blink quickly, and his body freezes in place as The Viper swings the pickaxe over his head and splits the miner's skull. As the kindly miner collapses to the ground, his last words having been spoken, and The Viper tells his brothers to bury the man's body at the cave's entrance. The last words Henry Trudgeon hears are The Radish's question: "Do you think that mule really can smell gold?"

WEDNESDAY, JULY 10

EVERYONE IS STILL TALKING about the ferocious grizzly as we feast on its remains. The banks of North Bridger Creek are far more pleasant than our surroundings the past several days, and I listen to the calming babble of moving water as I eat. The hearty stew is most welcome, but I can't help thinking of the pillaging barbarian. It's hard to believe I was close enough to a grizzly bear to smell its putrid breath. Though, at the time, I hadn't noticed the rancid smell of death and decay that accompanied the attack. Now, the memory singes my nostrils.

Alvah and Lucky have joined us for supper. They sit beside the fire long after everyone is done eating and the children have wandered off. Only Christopher remains, seated beside Alvah. Since Lucky joined the wagon train, Christopher hasn't seemed himself. The seasoned mountain man tells exciting stories of his wilderness adventures, and Christopher is captivated by them, but he seems like an unwatered flower in a forgotten pot. It's understandable that Lucky would occupy all of Alvah's time, yet Christopher feels left out.

As I move about camp, I feel like Lucky is always watching me, even though he never actually looks at me straight on. It's like his eyes are stuck looking out the corners, covertly observing everything I do. Does he think I don't notice? Am I a curiosity to him, is he attracted to me, or is there something else on his mind?

Alvah says that his father is afraid of white women. Whenever I speak to Lucky, he seems tongue-tied. He's always polite but looks to my side when speaking to me. It's as if he is afraid of what will happen if he lets his eyes meet mine. I might take it personally, however, I've noticed he does the same when talking with other women, though I haven't noticed him looking at other women from the corners of his eyes.

I call to Christopher and ask him to join me. When we get to the stream, I ask him if he will stand watch while I clean the dirty supper dishes. He says, "That bear's got you spooked, Mama. Don't it?"

My head nods, and I smile at my son. The real reason I brought him is so that Alvah and Lucky can talk without the weight of a child's ears hanging at the edge of their conversation. I ask Christopher how his arm is doing.

As I scrub encrusted bear meat from the skillet's bottom, Christopher chucks rocks into the water with his good arm. When the dishes are clean, I ask Christopher if he can collect firewood one-handed. Then I return to camp.

I don't mean to eavesdrop, but I can't help stopping to listen from beside the wagon. I'm surprised that the father has taken this long to tell the son about his family.

Edith was bossy, but Lucky was content to always do what she told him. Lucky explains, "She was a pretty girl, but I was afraid to talk to her."

Growing up, Lucky spent all of his time with his grandfather and uncle, a seaman named Thomas. The old man was a widower, and Thomas was a bachelor. Lucky never spent any time with women or girls. Lucky explains, "After a couple of years in the mountains, I returned home for a visit. Edith became a beautiful woman, almost as pretty as Dorcas, and I wanted to make her my wife, though I didn't know how to talk to her."

I can't help but touch my lips. Why has Lucky mentioned my name when discussing his son's mother? What's more, Lucky called me *pretty*. That's hardly the word I would use to describe myself. I tell myself I shouldn't be listening in on their conversation, but remain in place.

Lucky continues. "Edith didn't care. She wasn't interested in wilderness life and was happy to talk for both of us. It pained me to think of giving up the mountains, but I convinced myself I would be happy married to Edith and working in a warehouse on the docks."

The seasoned mountain man rubs the salt and pepper whiskers on his chin and looks toward the sky above the wagons. "I'm not proud of what happened before the wedding. Edith said it was common for engaged couples to be together before marriage. We spent a couple of long afternoons in the hayloft of a big barn. On our wedding day, I arrived at church an hour early. I stood there all day, but she never showed up. The next morning, I saddled up and rode back to the mountains. I've never gone back. I never knew what became of Edith. I don't know why, but it never occurred to me that she might have had a baby. Now, I wonder, what if she regretted not marrying me? What if she looked for me when she learned she was pregnant?"

Alvah says, "I don't know. Mother said that you died at sea, just as your father did. Grandfather told me that Mother got cold feet, but a few days later, the two of you eloped before you set sail, never to return. She lived as a widow. I never knew that I was a bastard child." I can't discern how Alvah feels as he voices the word *bastard*.

The subject of their conversation changes quickly. Lucky says, "I can always tell when bears are near, particularly grizzly bears. It's a useful gift to have when you're a mountain man. I must have been distracted. I should have known that the monster was close by. Between finding you and thoughts of that bewitching woman, I just ain't myself."

Alvah says, "You mean Dorcas? Mrs. Moon? Are you smitten then?" I remind myself it would be a good idea to slink away, but don't.

Lucky chuckles in a low voice. "Smitten. I guess that's a good word for it. I don't know what to say to a white woman. Any woman, I guess. Instead of talking all the time, why can't white women just slip beneath a man's blankets at night? Dang sight better idea than having a courtship and wedding. But Mrs. Moon, I don't know. She's not like Edith or my Indian wives."

I can't believe that I'm standing here listening to this conversation and I am shocked by what Lucky says. I should step forward and tell him that I don't plan to marry again, but then I'd have to admit eavesdropping. I can feel the heat in my cheeks as I imagine slipping beneath Lucky's blankets in the middle of the night. I remember fantasizing that Alvah was older so that we could be together. Why should I not consider his father, given the man seems 'smitten' as he says? The Nye men are precisely the sort that catch a woman's eye. However, I prefer lithe men over muscular ones, like the lissome antelope-eyed assistant wagon master with the curious accent.

Something catches the corner of my eye, and I glance to my right. Agapito leans against the corner of Boss Wheel's wagon, his presence almost blending into the twilight shadows. He's watching me listen to Lucky and Alvah's conversation, and suddenly, our eyes lock. A flush of heat races through me, causing my palms and underarms to grow uncomfortably sweaty. I blink furiously and then look away, wondering whether he can hear their low voices. Feeling devious and deceitful, I turn away from Agapito's unsettling gaze, a pang of guilt piercing through me. I retreat to the river, pretending to busy myself with the already clean skillet, wishing I could erase my intrusion on a quiet, personal discussion.

Maybe it would be easier to accept gentleman callers than to keep trying to avoid them. Good Heavens, what does Agapito think of me now, with my awkwardness on full display? A bead of sweat trickles down my back. It isn't like we can be together, even if he were inclined to want to romance me.

THURSDAY, JULY 11

AFTER A SWEATY JOURNEY of more than twenty miles, we reach the impressive Bear River. The wide waterway cuts a greener swath through the desert than the creeks we've grown accustomed to.

When supper is finished, Lucky and Alvah set up targets beyond the wagons. Following the monstrous bruin's midnight attack, and with continued worry about outlaws ahead, it isn't just the men who take an interest in our self-defense. Even the ladies, some of whom reluctantly attended Agapito's shooting class outside of Independence, are determined to learn how to hit the middle of the target. Thinking back to our first campground, it seems like years ago rather than only a couple of months.

One would think that we had nothing better to do than idle away the hours, and an unlimited supply of ammunition. I leave the guns to others who need more practice than I do. Arikta has set up a secondary target nearby. I walk over, and he hands me a bow. "Would you like to try archery, ma'am?"

I shrug. "Why not? Do you think you could teach me, Arikta?"

He says, "I expect so." He nocks an arrow into his bowstring, pulls it back, and sends the projectile flying straight toward the middle of a charcoal circle sketched onto an old deerskin. After the demonstration, he says, "You try now, yes?"

The bow feels good in my right hand. I copy Arikta's movements, and as I prepare to shoot, he steps forward and lifts my right arm slightly. "Aim a little above, ma'am." Then, the young man steps away. "Pull back as far as you can."

My arrow pierces the target a short distance from Arikta's. I hadn't realized that people were watching, but a group of curious bystanders cheer my shot. I notice Lucky looking directly at me, but he turns away, looking to my right when I glance at him. Then, I turn away and see Agapito carrying a stump, followed by Dembi Koofai, who has a couple of axes.

It looks like we're preparing for war, but I can't resist following Agapito and the Shoshone scout. Agapito smiles at me and says, "Remember when you told me about your axe-throwing skills, *estimada*?"

I'm impressed by his memory and touched that he remembered that moment. I say, "I hoped that you had forgotten. Tossing cleavers ain't exactly ladylike, but I guess you know by now, I'm not much of a lady."

Agapito says, "You keep saying that, and I do not know why. Who is to say what makes a lady? Is it up to her or those who catch her eye?"

"Goodness gracious, Agapito." I can't help feeling flustered by what he has said. It's unclear who he is referring to, and there are far too many people around us to clarify the matter. Whatever does he mean by *those who catch her eye?* I try to change the subject. Instead of denying my expertise,

I take the opposite approach. How long has it been since I've done this? Thinking back to my childhood, I stand confidently and boast, "Shall I show you how it is done?"

"Yes, *estimada*. I was hoping that you would do just that."

When my first throw lands smack dab in the middle of the heavy log, Agapito says, "That is a lucky throw, yes? You must do it again."

I look at him and say, "Lucky throw, you say? Oh, I see how it is."

Dembi Koofai runs the axe back to me.

My second throw lands where my first toss did. I look at Agapito and say, "Maybe the target isn't far enough away."

Agapito laughs and motions to Dembi Koofai, who moves the log back. "Can you hit that, *estimada*?"

"We shall see. I love a challenge." I throw the chopper and hit the log. It's a little to the side of its center and high, but it has connected. Onlookers clap and cheer, and I place my hand over my face. Once again, I imagine myself as Joan of Arc and wish I were just a *little* more ladylike.

Agapito, who likes to get a crowd's attention, shouts, "Who else would like to try? Can anyone else hit the log? It is very far, no?"

I step back and look over at the archery station. Alvah and Lucky take turns drawing bowstrings and firing at the target. Christopher looks on with a frown. I know he'd like nothing better than to learn how to use a bow and arrow, but it's impossible with his arm in a sling.

Looking back at Agapito, I catch the faint glimpse of a frown. Is it because I glanced in Lucky's direction? I don't recall seeing such an expression on his face before. He quickly rebounds and cheerfully says, "We have many ways to defend ourselves if the outlaws come for us, no?"

I can't help but worry. "Do you think there's danger ahead?"

"I cannot say. I wish I could, *estimada*." He turns his head slightly, and I look deep into his eyes. He says, "We will do everything we can to keep you greenhorns safe." The corners of his mouth turn upward as he says the word *greenhorns*.

Before nightfall, Lucky teaches us how to fight with knives. Instead of daggers, combatants circle one another with long feathers. I watch as Bobby and Wayne take their turn. Telling myself that they are practicing, and that their altercation is make-believe doesn't keep me from clenching my jaws, leaning forward, and putting my hands on my hips. With those two, one can never tell what might happen. They make a good show of pretending that the fringed quills are real and that their battle is high stakes, and it takes great effort to convince myself not to intervene. The rest of the crowd, however, chortles and guffaws at the sight of the best friends as they grapple and stab at each other.

If Lucky's instruction weren't so necessary, perhaps I would find the humor in the situation. As the young men wrestle playfully on the ground, Bobby begins to laugh as if he were being tickled with the fluffy end of Wayne's feather. The laughter becomes infectious, and Wayne rolls off of Bobby. Before long, both combatants are incapacitated by uncontrollable, side-splitting, fits of laughter. Bobby laughs so hard, tears stream from his eyes, and Wayne stops laughing only long enough to complain that his cheeks hurt.

Judgmentally, I shake my head and turn away. I should be glad their mock battle didn't escalate to a real fight. I've always hated watching men fight.

FRIDAY, JULY 12

WHEN WE ARE SETTLED into camp at Smiths Fork on the Bear River, I cross the circled wagons to Alvah's camp. I catch Lucky there alone and try to engage him in conversation. I am determined to help him conquer his fear of talking to women. I pepper him with easy questions and step to his right when he answers, since he always looks over my shoulder when he speaks to me.

After twenty minutes of stilted conversation that goes in circles, I give up and return to my wagon. Perhaps there is no changing a man who is so set in his ways. Why should I care if the man can't talk to women? He's managed to get along this far without so doing.

When I return to our wagons, I'm pleased to see that the children have gathered a large quantity of wood. I glance around, looking for Rose, and think, *Oh no, not again.* I ask, "Does anyone know where Rose is?"

Stillman answers. "We split up to gather wood. She hasn't returned yet." I look at the sun and estimate how long we have before it sets. While Andrew and Stillman grease the axles, I whip up a batch of peppermint scones. If Rose hasn't returned by the time I'm done, we'll have to sound the alarm. I'm not looking forward to asking the wagon master to conduct yet another search for my wayward daughter.

My worries are interrupted by an unexpected visit. Charlotte clutches Hollis' elbow, wide smiles on their faces. Just behind them, Violet clings to PBJ. The young man nods and grins at me. My children gather closely beside me.

Charlotte releases Hollis' arm and her expression is radiant. She looks as if she might burst, and says, "Go on, Violet. Tell them the news."

Charlotte's daughter doesn't need to say a word. After watching the young couple's romantic strolls each night, I'm sure that everyone in our rolling village anticipated that the young couple would wed somewhere along the way to Oregon.

I shake PBJ's hand, kiss Violet's cheek, and embrace Charlotte. From within our hug, Charlotte whispers into my ear. "I'm so delighted, Dorcas. I just wish my Martin were here to see his sister get married." As we step away from each other, Charlotte wipes a tear from the corner of her eye and sniffles. To the small crowd, she says, "Violet told you that she and PBJ are getting married, but what she didn't say is that tomorrow is the day."

PBJ says, "We can't wait any longer." He turns to Violet and says, "Are you sure you don't want to get married right now?"

Violet says, "We were meant to be together."

Hollis interjects. "I have given PBJ my blessing, but if they insist on getting married tonight, I shall revoke my consent."

PBJ tips his head forward and says, "Reckon we can wait another day."

As quickly as PBJ and the Appleyard family arrived, they're off to spread their joyful news. As they depart, I tell myself that I'm glad for the young couple. Truthfully, I'm a little envious. Then I think of Charlotte, and how happy she is about her daughter's engagement. When a young couple's marriage is meant to be, it's a blessing for the entire family.

A foul odor dislodges dreamy romantic thoughts from my mind. My scones! They're burned. With a disappointed grumble, I think about how we cannot afford to waste food, but who can eat lumps of charcoal?

Rose appears just as I remove the Dutch oven from the embers. She approaches slowly from the north. There's something different about her. I'm accustomed to seeing a blank expression on her face. Usually, she steps like she's sleepwalking. Today she seems equally oblivious, but even from a distance, her eyes seem to sparkle.

When Rose gets near enough to hear me, I say, "There you are, honey. Where have you been, Rose?"

She turns her face toward me, and the twinkle in her eye suddenly ignites. I didn't mean to sound accusatory. Her fiery expression comes with an angry growl. It seems she has no intention of telling me where she's been, and I'm surprised by her reaction, though her unwillingness to tell me where she's been is not startling.

Then, I notice the choker at her neck. It would be hard to overlook such a unique adornment. If she wants to keep secrets, wearing such an object will not help her cause. Three rows of brilliant, hairpipe bones separated by dark red beads, circle her neck. Just above her sternum, there's a large, wooden charm. I gulp when I realize that the horrible pendant features an intricately carved wolf's head with bared teeth. I gasp, "Good heavens, Rose. What is that?"

Rose stomps, huffs furiously, and makes a sound like, "Ugh" or "argh," and then tells me to mind my own business. Her hands ball into fists, and she turns away, disappearing into the wagon. I look at Stillman and the children, but nobody says anything. From the looks on their faces, I gather they're as confused as I am. I should not have questioned her in front of them.

Rose's typically dreary countenance has turned hostile. I shudder at the thought of an angry wolf at her throat. Then it hits me. Rose must have a beau. But who could it be? She's too young. Should I forbid it? I glance to my left and see Dembi Koofai leaning against the master's wagon, and notice that he appears to be looking in our direction. That's it! Dembi Koofai is romancing Rose, and he must have given her the choker. Doesn't he know about Boss Wheel's rule against courting the wagon train's women?

Why won't my daughter confide in me? I remember what it's like to be lovesick, and thirteen. If only I could understand why she's become combative. Does she think I would not accept Dembi Koofai as her eventual or potential husband? Other than her age, the only thing I have trouble with is the wolf at her throat. I'm surprised Dembi Koofai didn't carve a cedar scorpion instead. I wish he had.

A strange question forms in my mind. *What would Larkin do? What would Larkin say?* Of course, he would say that Rose will work it out on her own, just as he claimed Rose would get over her preoccupation with death. *Why did Larkin have to go and die, leaving me to deal with this alone?* Self pity never did anybody any good. I must not think about Larkin like that.

Will Rose's new romance displace the dark cloud that has hung over her for so long? Maybe the dark cloud was better than the angry demeanor she now exhibits.

My racing mind has leaped far into the future. Rose will not find it easy to be the wife of an Indian, but I don't have a problem with it. Love is strange, and there's no explanation for what makes one person love another. Sometimes, opposites are drawn to one another. Other times, very similar people pair up. I guess that Rose is comparable to the mysterious Shoshone scout. If only I didn't have to look at the canid at her sternum. If only Rose were a couple of years older.

When I glance back into the wagon master's camp, the young Indian is gone.

It's dark, and I look beyond the wagons. I feel a prickle at the back of my neck. Why do I have the feeling that somebody is watching me?

SATURDAY, JULY 13

WE FORCE OUR WELL-WORN wagons through steep muddy hills and reach Thomas Fork at Bear River early in the afternoon. Sharp riverbanks make crossing the smaller river difficult. Despite the challenge posed by the terrain, wood and water are plentiful, and it's nice to camp in a fertile valley.

Everyone looks forward to Violet and PBJ's wedding this evening and a well-deserved day off tomorrow. Shortly after the wagons circle as we work to dispense with the day's chores, I look for Rose.

When I look to the north, I see her thin figure tiptoeing away on the opposite side of Thomas Fork. She has her arms pulled toward her chest, and her body hunches forward. Usually, when she wanders off, she seems oblivious to her surroundings. Today, it looks like she is sneaking off intentionally.

I take a few steps northward. What should I do? A lady wouldn't permit her daughter to venture off like this. Dottie Crouse's voice appears in my head, warning that it isn't proper behavior for a young woman to be alone with a man until after marriage. I think back to when I followed Noah into the woods. Was I was older than Rose is now? It's hard to recall.

I'm tempted to follow, but what would I do when I catch up with her? The urge to spy is strong, but what good would it do to confirm my suspicions? I've had the talk a woman needs to have with her daughter——several times, for the sake of caution. I could read her diary. I remember the many times I've been tempted to do so. Countless times, I have wondered why Rose doesn't confide in me. I'm sure that she would find me sympathetic. Everyone else does. Why shouldn't she?

A swift glance into the wagon master's camp confirms Dembi Koofai's absence. Just because he is gone doesn't mean Rose sneaked off to see *him*. I remember, a few weeks ago, thinking about the Knox boy from Carolina who travels with his aunts. There was something about the way the boy talked to Rose that made me wonder. I quickly dismiss the thought. There's no way that Garland Knox would present Rose with an Indian choker. Then, I see Garland leading a pair of oxen toward the herd.

I tell myself that I will follow Rose in fifteen minutes, but I keep putting it off. It's hard to tell how long fifteen minutes is anyway. We used to keep time by asking Larkin, who would sometimes become irritated when we too often implored him to check the time for us. I think of him pulling his pocket watch from his waistcoat. There is a pang in my gut. I think, *I could use your help now, Larkin.*

Ultimately, I decide to let Rose return to camp in her own time. That *is* what Larkin would advise, I'm sure of it, only I don't know what he would have thought about having an Indian for a son-in-law, or having his daughter married so young. I chide myself for jumping to conclusions and rushing fears of Rose's wedding. Just because she has a beau doesn't mean that wedding plans are imminent.

On the other hand, eighteen-year-old Pious Bull Jr. stands at The Hub. People have flocked to the center of the circle. Twin fiddles fill the air with music, and seventeen-year-old Violet emerges from within Dr. Appleyard's wagon. Hollis leads his daughter through the crowd, and I jog to the mother of the groom's side. Charlotte looks radiant, the best she's seemed since Martin tragically shot himself at Ash Hollow, back in May.

As Reverend Meadows joins PBJ and Violet Appleyard, I watch the clouds gather above us. I don't believe in omens, but I think of Oona Reid and wonder whether we should expect rain. I whisper to Andrew, who stands beside me. He confirms that it will rain, and I can taste a sour frown forming on my face.

The wedding party is festive despite the transitioning weather. The fiddles wail, and guests line up to dance a reel. Andrew and Christopher dance with Hannah and Miranda Knox. Stillman holds Dahlia Jane in his arms, and pretends to waltz with her. I fade through the crowd and glance to the north. I wish that Rose would return.

I'm surprised by a man's hand on my waist. Instinct closes my eyes as I turn toward him, and the man's lips touch mine. I realize that my head tilts up rather than down. The firm kiss is unlike any other I can recall. When it's over, I open my eyes, look up and see Lucky Nye. For a fraction of a second, I see into the deep pools of his pale blue eyes before he looks to his right, over my shoulder, and says. "I don't know what came over me, ma'am. I guess I got caught up in the moment. It's been *years* since I kissed a woman." The mountain man wishes me a pleasant evening, and is gone.

What should I make of what has happened? I touch my lips and remember Captain Meadows saying that a woman alone can't be choosy. I love Alvah like a son, but could I love the man's father as a husband? What if he never learned how to talk to me or look me in the eyes? He's not the man I long for, but there's no chance of marrying Agapito. I remind myself that I intend to remain a woman alone.

A commotion stirs near my right elbow.

Wayne says to Bobby, "Dorcas is right. Your curly beard is butt-ugly."

"Least I can grow a respectable beard."

It is just as I feared. The combative friends have been drinking again, and their rivalry has combusted. If it weren't one thing to set them off, it would be another. I'm lost in thought and memories. I miss seeing who throws the first punch. They should know by now that I will not hesitate for long. If only they were fighting with feathers again, instead of fists. Perhaps I should let them work it out for themselves, but I can't stand by idly.

I cross my arms for a minute and let them pound each other a few times. Hopefully, they'll learn a lesson. Then, I bend at the waist, grab Bobby's shirt just as Wayne's meat hook clobbers *my* chin, spins my head, and drops me to the ground.

As it turns out, that's a faster way to stop men from fighting than my usual method. Bobby grabs one hand, Wayne grabs the other, and they lift me back to my feet. I pat my jaw with my fingers and look at Wayne. The young man apologizes profusely and begs forgiveness. I slap his shoulder and tell him not to worry, but make him promise not to fight anymore, at least not tonight.

When I turn away from Bobby and Wayne, I see Rose sneaking back into camp. I walk toward our wagon, hoping to meet her as the Heavens open wide and a torrential downpour soaks the celebrating travelers.

The almost spontaneous wedding is over, and everyone piles into wagons, seeking cover beneath canvas. We huddle together in close quarters, and I look at Rose. There's a long furry hairdrop woven within her stringy locks. The look on her face seems to warn me. I hear unspoken words in my head. *Not one word. Don't you dare say a thing.*

SUNDAY, JULY 14

LAST NIGHT'S STORM IS long gone. I'm the first to awaken, and it's nice to amble about in the morning. Many complain about the time we waste laying by on Sundays, but I find it a welcome respite.

I spark a fire and set the speckled pot at its edge. My mind races from Lucky's surprise kiss, to yesterday's wedding, to Rose's strange behavior, and my jaw smarts where Wayne Horton's meaty paw struck me. I smell bacon and look over to the master's camp. Agapito waves, and I stroll over with my empty tin cup in hand.

"Good morning, Dorcas. I have extra coffee here if you do not want to wait for yours."

I crouch beside him and extend my empty cup toward him, grimacing as the scabs on my thigh crackle. I say, "Your coffee tastes better than mine does anyway."

As Agapito pours, he says, "You have a very expressive face, *estimada*."

"Good Heavens, whatever do you mean?" Nobody has ever told me that before.

Agapito says, "When I look at you, I can usually tell what you are thinking by the look on your face. You worry when you look at Rose. You are proud when you look at Andrew, and when you look at Christopher, you almost look envious, wishing you could be more like him, I think, no? When you look at your baby girl, you look like you want to pinch her cheeks and smother her in your arms."

I take a sip of coffee from the hot cup's brim and say, "I guess I *must* have an expressive face then."

Agapito's nostrils flare, and his eyebrows pinch together. "The way you look at the lucky mountain man, I do not know. I can not tell what you think when you look at him." He sounds more than curious, but not quite accusing, and I guess I don't know what he's thinking, any more than he knows my thoughts. I touch my lips and look into Agapito's eyes.

The man pokes at the fire with a thick stick, stirring the coals. He says, "I should not mention that I saw him kiss you. It surprised you, yes? I do not have the right to be jealous, but it makes me mad. I am sorry, *estimada*. It is not your burden."

I say, "Burden?" If anyone knows the heavy weight of love, I think it is me. My heart races. I stifle the desire to confess my deep feelings for him at the same time as the realization that Agapito is jealous of Lucky confuses my tongue.

Agapito looks at me while he speaks. "Yes, *estimada*. I speak of my promise to Merced and Boss Wheel's strict rules."

I say, "Oh, I understand." He is jealous, but then he says that we can't be together. I force myself to speak with confidence. "I have decided to remain a woman alone rather than remarry, anyway. Instead of love, I dedicate myself to friendships and helping people in need." We look at each other, but no more words come to either of us.

I recall when I stood on top of Independence Rock and fantasized that I was Athena. I felt a tremendous surge of power, like there was nothing I couldn't do. There's probably only one man in the world who could change my mind now, but there doesn't seem to be the slightest chance for us. Too much stands in our way, I suppose. It briefly occurs to me that if I love the man, I should fight for him, rules and promises to the departed be damned.

Why does it seem that some people find love so easily? It's like building fires in the morning and at night. Some days, the tinder takes the spark quickly and the kindling rapidly blazes into an inferno. In contrast, sometimes it takes way too long to get a fire going, even when the weather cooperates and the wood is dry. Is it fair that PBJ and Violet have easily found love and now are joined in holy matrimony, their union blessed by God, Reverend Meadows, and witnessed by a village full of fellow travelers? They say their love was meant to be, as if predestined, preordained, but what about the rest of us? Why do the stars align for so few lovers?

Bacon sizzles loudly in the skillet beyond Agapito's knees, spitting grease, and I wonder if it's burning. I say, "I think the bacon is cooked, Agapito."

He hops toward the pan with a thick cloth protecting his hand. He gasps, "*Gracias, estimada*. I must have been distracted."

I return to my feet, and my knees crack. I take another sip and say, "I feel like an aunt, big sister, or cousin to Alvah, and I wanted to make his father feel welcome. Lucky has difficulty speaking to women, so I've tried to befriend him. I suppose he misunderstands my intentions."

Agapito stands beside me. "I suspect you are right, *estimada*. I could not help overhearing Lucky say to Alvah, 'Why does she not just slip under my blankets after dark?' I do not believe he is accustomed to courting a woman."

I roll my eyes and say, "Goodness, gracious. I guess he *has* gotten the wrong idea." I rub my chin and say, "He is an attractive man, but I could do without the bramble on his chin."

Agapito rubs his cheeks and shows me his dimples. I shake my head and feel myself blushing. Our conversation is interrupted by the arrival of hungry scouts beside Agapito's fire. I should leave them, but can't help lingering.

Arikta is disappointed that they did not find game. Everybody would welcome fresh meat.

Mostly, I focus my attention on Dembi Koofai. He's normally evasive and hard to read. Agapito told me I have an expressive face, but his Shoshone scout most certainly does not. It occurs to me, why don't I just ask Dembi Koofai if he and Rose are sweet on each other? The silent, smoldering types are unpredictable. Would Dembi Koofai be angry? Would he confess his love for Rose to me, or would he deny it? I keep telling myself that I would not object, but for the fact that Rose is so young.

Dembi Koofai says to Agapito. "Somethin' isn' righ'."

The assistant wagon master seeks to clarify. "What do you mean?"

"I can' explain. Outside of camp, when we hun', feels like we are the prey. I always know. Can' find no tracks."

My eyes shift back and forth between the men. It isn't just me. I'm not the only one that has a sense of being stalked. Dembi Koofai can feel it too.

Monday, July 15

Rather than follow the Bear River south and then north again, the trail leads west across a steep hill. After only five miles, we are forced to make camp along pencil thin Sheep Creek, due to Grace Weaver's labor.

Other than the meager trickle of water and a narrow ribbon of short grass, there isn't much to the topography. After setting up camp, I look around for Rose, who has gone missing, yet again. Andrew tells me that she wandered north along the creek.

I glance into the master's camp. I don't see Dembi Koofai either, and decide to hike along the creek. After about a mile, the waterway trickles northeast between steep hills. A half a mile farther, I find Rose on her knees in front of a large sage, beside the rill. It is hard to see what she is doing until I draw nearer.

Rose doesn't notice my presence. I'm not trying to conceal myself. Except for the occasional twiggy shrub, there's nothing behind which to hide anyway. When I'm twenty feet away, I stop and watch as it appears she's performing some sort of ritual. A flicker of doubt and the image of a fairy tale witch crosses my mind before I tell myself that such thoughts are ridiculous.

With a small knife that I didn't know she possessed, Rose cuts sprigs from the sagebrush and sets them on the ground in front of her. Then, she places her hands together with a branchlet between them, and rolls the twig back and forth across her palms. She holds her hands near her face, and it looks like she's inhaling the scent. Next, she sets the woody little branch down and runs her fingers slowly through her hair. Finally, her fingers massage her scalp. It is as if she thinks she's sudsing soap.

Normally, Rose doesn't like to undress in my presence, or when there is a chance that anyone might see her, so I'm surprised when she disrobes, and I turn to the east. She still doesn't notice my presence, though I haven't been behind her for a long while. It is as if she is oblivious to her surroundings, and can't see beyond the sage in front of her.

From time to time, I glance at Rose from the corner of my eye. I think of Dembi Koofai who always seems to observe the world obliquely, and Lucky who doesn't look at me directly. Rose continues dry washing herself in the aroma of sage, and I remember the many occasions when she collected the shrubbery, filling the pockets of her dress with it.

Rose's thin body is always concealed beneath her oversized, plum-colored dress. Though she hasn't seemed to inherit my ample bosom, I realize that Rose has matured. Despite the dark world she inhabits, there's no denying that my daughter is blossoming.

After Rose dons her familiar dress, she carefully weaves the fuzzy hairdrop between her tresses. Then, she returns the choker to her neck. Her fingers touch the carving, carefully centering it at her throat. Thinking of the realistic depiction of a wolf makes me tremble, and I try to distract myself by looking back to the west.

I'm surprised that Rose still doesn't recognize my proximity to her. Having completed her ablution, she continues along the banks of the narrow rivulet. After a while, she stops and scans the horizon. It looks like she's searching for something in the distance, and I wonder what she expects to see. Then, it occurs to me. Perhaps she's looking for Dembi Koofai. Did Rose tiptoe away from camp, hoping to secretly meet the man?

What should I do? I've been nearby so long, it seems strange to suddenly call out to Rose. I don't want to leave her here in the expansive wilderness, all alone, and I'm not sure that I'd be happier to have her accompanied if that means leaving her alone with a fully mature man. I gently bite my lip, and prepare to speak as Rose turns and returns along the waterway, back toward camp.

I stand and watch as Rose makes her way back through the desiccated canyon. Rather than follow her, I remain. I could use a little time to myself as well. There's so much to think about. My conversation with Agapito last night lingers in my head, and I haven't decided what to say to Lucky Nye. It's been a few days now since he kissed me. Should I bring it up and discourage him, or let it drop? Maybe I should prepare words to say if it should happen again.

Then, Rose returns to my thoughts. How could she not have seen me? I wasn't hiding my presence. It's as if I've become invisible to her. When I was her age, I was often lost in my thoughts, and they always centered around my dreams of Noah, but I don't think I was ever so consumed by fantasy that I was oblivious to my surroundings. Perhaps the dark thoughts that seem to consume her are different. I'm sure she would be the first to say that I don't understand. When we are that age, we don't believe that adults were every young themselves.

I amble forward, a couple of hundred feet farther along Sheep Creek. I'm surprised when I see the black Appaloosa emerge from a draw ahead of me, and a nervous tinge tickles my belly. The appearance of Dembi Koofai on Coffeepot confirms my suspicions. The young Indian dismounts when he reaches me and gestures toward the limp body of a dead antelope, draped over Coffeepot's back.

What should I say to this man? He is not fluent in English. Though I think he understands most words, he's not very good at speaking his thoughts. He doesn't seem to be disappointed to find me here instead of Rose. Perhaps she intended to surprise him. Maybe they hadn't planned to meet here this afternoon. I compliment his hunting skills and then tiptoe into dangerous territory by bringing up my daughter. I can feel and hear my voice quaver as I say, "That's a lovely necklace that Rose wears."

"Is ver' nice. Ver' rich." The taciturn young man conveys nothing more than approval for the ornament. I wonder about his use of the word *rich*. Does he mean that the choker is valuable?

"It looks like someone spent a lot of time making the necklace. She almost looks like an Indian when she wears it."

He says, "She like the Indian?"

I'm not sure what he means by *the Indian*. Does he refer to the race, or a specific individual? Is he asking whether she likes him in particular? I say, "I think she does."

He says, "You like the Indian?"

Again, I'm not sure what I'm saying when I answer, "I do." The young man is dark and mysterious. He's tall and handsome, and I can understand Rose's interest in him. I wonder if Dembi Koofai understands Boss Wheel's rules and how they would apply to him and Rose.

As I wrestle with what to say to Dembi Koofai about meeting privately with Rose, he motions down the river. "Now I go. Don' stay alone here." He leaps effortlessly onto his horse and trots off through the ravine.

When he's gone, I begin to make my way back along the creek. Nothing Dembi Koofai said directly confirms it, but I'm convinced that he and Rose are keeping company. If only she were a little older and he were a little younger, I'd feel much better about the situation.

TUESDAY, JULY 16

I AWAKEN WITH A start and see the fully illuminated wagon bonnet above me. Why didn't the trumpet sound before sunrise? We should be marching up the landmark to the west of us, known as Big Hill.

The children have finished the morning's chores when I join them beside the fire. Stillman explains, "Mrs. Weaver still has not had her baby."

The poor woman has labored all day, then all night, and still, her baby hasn't come. I can't help thinking of Jennie. Childbirth is difficult enough without having to bring forth life in the wilderness, along the trail.

Stillman says, "Some of the men claim we should continue without the Weavers and let them catch up next Sunday. It's only the middle of July, but they are afraid of getting caught in the mountains like the Donner party."

I say, "We can't leave anyone behind, Stillman. How barbaric? Who said we should leave the Weavers behind?"

Stillman shrugs. "Galusha said it. Samuel nodded in agreement, and Horace thinks we are all going to die no matter what we do. I think others agree we shouldn't stop, but Captain Meadows says it wouldn't be right to leave the Weavers or to make her labor in a moving wagon."

I'm not accustomed to agreeing with Captain Meadows, but in this case, I do. "He is right, Stillman. If they go, we're staying with the Weavers." Though we've been traveling together for months, I don't know them well. I have nothing against them; I guess our paths don't often cross. I try to recall anything about the young couple. All I can remember is that Grace is a sister of Sarah Terwilliger, whose husband was killed by outlaws last year.

Hours later, I wander across the circle to Alvah Nye's wagon and find Lucky, alone near a small fire. After he tells me that Alvah is hunting, he says, "We're almost out of wood and there's none nearby. No buffalo chips, neither."

I say, "We can spare some. We put up extra at Thomas Fork."

"We'd be obliged. I'll fill your box on the other side of the hill." As always, Lucky avoids making eye contact. The polite mountain man offers me a cup of coffee, and I accept.

When we're seated side by side, I ask about his family. "At Fort Bridger, you said all your children were breeds."

Talking *about* women makes Lucky almost as nervous as talking *to* them. The big man's limbs retreat beneath the stripes of his festive jorongo, like a turtle pulling its appendages into a shell. "I had a Brulé woman several years ago. Our daughter lives with her grandmother."

I say, "That's why I saw you in Spotted Tail's village. What's your daughter's name?"

"She calls herself Penny. She's the same age as your daughter, Rose. Almost a woman now."

"I had a Lemhi woman also. Our daughter, Bia Maswiki, lives with her mother's sister. She's seven-years-old, and quite a chatterbox."

I repeat the musical name, wondering how it should be spelled. "Bia Maswiki."

Lucky holds up his hand and wiggles his digits. "It means big fingers. I guess she takes after me."

"What do you mean by *Had a woman?* Were they not your wives?"

"Some trappers don't think of Indian women as wives, but many do. To me, they are."

"If you don't mind me asking, what happened to them?"

"Both died of illnesses. I'm not known for having good luck, and I guess it rubbed off."

"Why are you called *Lucky*, then?"

"Everybody's called me that since I was a sprout. Because I'm the 13th Alvah Nye in succession, I bear the curse of an unlucky number. I never imagined I'd pass that name to a son of mine."

I'm slow to realize what this means. "So, your son, Alvah Nye, he is actually Alvah Nye, the 14th? What a tradition. What an inheritance."

"You'd think we were royalty, but so far as I know, all of us been poor, hard-working folk, scratching out a living where we can."

After a long pause, I hesitate to ask the question I've been curious about. "Is there a reason you don't look at me when you speak?"

Lucky looks fast into my eyes, then quickly away. "No, ma'am. Just never was any women or girls around growing up, except for Edith." Lucky hunches over as if gazing at his reflection in the still surface of the black coffee in his tin cup.

The man beside me continues speaking. "Edith was a few years younger than me, but bossy. She could talk the ears off a mule. But I didn't mind. Long as she was talking, I didn't need to say anything. She wouldn't abide me disagreeing with her anyway, so I never bothered to try. I don't know whether I was already afraid of women before Edith, or whether Edith taught me to be afraid, but that's the way it's always been. My little Shoshone girl reminds me of her."

I'd like to know more about Edith. Instead, I inquire about his future plans. "You think you'll ever marry again, or take another woman as you say?"

"I don't reckon so, ma'am. Contrary to my name, I don't have any luck with romance."

I say, "Me neither."

Lucky casts a sideways glance at me. "Unlucky in love or won't marry again?"

"Both, I suppose."

"I see." Lucky takes a sip of coffee and swishes it around his mouth. He continues, "I guess I can get by on my own, with no company, but you seem like you need somebody 'round *you* if it's not too bold a' me to say so."

With more determination than I feel, I say the words I'm familiar saying to myself. "No, I shall remain a woman alone. I'll do as I want, without a man who needs tending or telling me what to do all the time."

"What if a man catches your eye?"

Lucky seems to have landed a blow at my point of doubt. "I guess a woman can change her mind. If I were to marry again, I would have to be sure it is true love. He would have to be a very patient, understanding sort of man. I ain't easy to love, don't you know?"

"Don't that sound like me?"

I knock a playful jab at Lucky's arm. "I think you'd be easy to love. You are certainly easy to look at. A woman could do far worse. You're a fine man, and I'm glad to have your friendship, but I don't think we're a match, you and me, Lucky. I'm sorry."

"You're a fine-looking woman, ma'am. You sure there isn't someone else?"

I'm not sure I am convincing myself as I say, "I don't suppose so." Then I repeat my intention to make it on my own.

After a week of begging, The Radish is granted a day away from watching over the trail. He can't wait to lead Flossie to the dark mountain to the north

of Birch Creek. If the friendly miner believed that the creature could smell gold, The Radish is inclined to believe also. It takes the young man all day to circle the prominence and explore everywhere a mule can be led. The Radish marks three spots where he is sure he sees Flossie smiling, like she did a week earlier when they met the doomed man and his talented mule.

When The Radish returns to the cabin, his brothers tell him about their day. Sloan and The Viper picked off a wagon that lagged its companions. The rig was loaded with liquor, some money, and not much else. The heavy whiskey exposed the teamster to a risk that The Viper was delighted to capitalize on.

The Viper isn't much of a drinker. When he drinks, he limits his intake to a single shot. Otherwise, he does not imbibe. On one occasion he drank to excess and realized that he couldn't stand losing control, even if just for a couple of hours or a single evening.

Sloan is delighted with the haul and encourages his little brother to celebrate with him. It doesn't take long for the underweight outlaws to have consumed more whiskey than they should.

The Viper takes advantage of the situation to question his brother. Controlling them depends on understanding what makes them tick. The Viper knows everything he needs to know about Sloan but isn't completely sure about The Radish.

The kid never seems to mind The Viper's probing questions, whereas Sloan frequently threatens to leave. The Radish never hesitates to tell his brothers about his dreams of finding gold and bedding hundreds of women. Aside from those objectives, The Radish has no opinion on how life should be lived.

After half a dozen slugs of whiskey, The Radish begins slurring his words. The Viper's invasive eyes lock with the Radish's and the interrogator says, "You don't really want to be an outlaw, do you, kid?"

The Radish's mouth bunches together. The 18-year-old shrugs and tells his brother that he's looking forward to retiring.

The Viper says, "Maybe you'll feel differently after you've had a taste of blood. Soon you will make your first kill." The Viper turns away and a tear forms in the corner of his eye. He can't remember the last time he cried. Why is it so easy to kill people, without emotion, yet the thought of his youngest brother doing so makes him melancholy?

WEDNESDAY, JULY 17

IT IS THE STRANGEST feeling. Ever since we departed Sheep Creek before sunrise, I've had the sense that someone is watching me. It is as if they hide behind a rock or tree, spying at me. Only, there isn't a rock or tree anywhere—just a big hump of mountain, known simply as Big Hill. Who named the waypoints on this trail? I'll never know.

Grace Weaver's baby finally came last night around midnight. Despite the long labor, Hollis and Charlotte Appleyard agree that mother and daughter are healthy. Though Hollis says it would be better if Grace had a day of rest, the consensus among travelers is that she will have to recover in the wagon as we continue our journey.

It has been a while since Rose walked backward as we traveled. Just when I think she's doing a bit better, she has a relapse and worry drops upon me, heavy as an anvil. Rose is no more aware of my presence today than when I followed her the day before yesterday. How can she be so unaware?

I'm glad to leave the bleak campground at Sheep Creek. If it weren't for the foreboding Big Hill to our west, there would be almost nothing to see except the sliver of a waterway, only deep enough to wash one's feet.

Sometimes the children complain of the boredom of walking mile upon mile down the trail, but I'd rather march than idle any longer on the eerie plain, east of Big Hill. What's more, something about the campsite is unsettling in a manner I can't quite put my finger on. It's the sort of place where one feels afraid of the dark, even when the sun shines brightly overhead. I don't think I am the only one that feels this way. I often have trouble getting Dahlia Jane to fall asleep, for fear of night terrors, and the last couple of nights have been worse than usual.

Today's journey is a challenge. This morning, we struggle to ascend, nudging oxen up along the high ridge. Whenever I stray a few feet from the wagon train, I'm surprised by movement near my feet. To look at the landscape, it would seem entirely barren, but all of the creatures that reside here are camouflaged so that they almost disappear.

When I lift a leg to step on a large stone, a long thin lizard whips its tail and scampers away. Instead of stepping there, I move my leg to step on a different rock. Another whiptail lizard suns itself there. They aren't particularly frightening, though I have no desire to crush one beneath my feet. We don't have any reptiles that look like these lizards back home. The dark brown lines of spots on tan colored skin, tiny bird-like claws, and double chins make the lizards look funny, but their beady little eyes get my attention. Could the feeling I have of being watched come from thousands of whiptail lizards?

Before our midday dinner, I step from the trail and hear the shake of a snake's rattle. We've grown accustomed to hearing such a sound, and I step away. The accusing eyes of the gold-colored rattler seem to want to speak to me, and I admonish myself for having such a ridiculous thought. Even if snakes could talk, this one wouldn't be able to. Its large triangular head has spread wide and hanging from the mouth that would be showing me fangs, dangles a long, spotted lizard tail. I can't help but admire the pattern and coloration of the flashy, six-foot-long reptile. At the same time, watching it consume the lizard makes me want to hork. I can almost hear the snake's warning in my head. "Leave me to my meal. I'll come for you later." Does this snake in particular have it out for me, or does he speak for his brothers and sisters elsewhere? What a thought to have. Reading the minds of animals is another thing I don't believe in.

I feel the sensation of bugs crawling across my skin. I brush the invisible insects away, but that doesn't stop the creepy feeling.

After dinner near the summit of Big Hill, we have a clear view of the western sky. A steep downward trail is as dangerous as an upward trail is tiring. Stillman thinks that the descent from Big Hill is as challenging as any we've faced yet. Earlier, we faced steep hills, but they were over more quickly. This long, sharp descent takes hours.

At one point, I look away from the straining oxen, tired of watching them struggle to keep our heavy wagon from pushing them down the hill. I squint into the hot, shimmering summer air. Something beneath a large sagebrush catches my eye, and I can't help but step forward to get a closer look. I stop dead in my tracks when I realize what I see is a wolf taking advantage of the dappled shade of the scraggly, fragrant branches.

The wolf gets to his feet and stands menacingly. Its ears tip back, and its nose points downward. Hostile yellow eyes look directly at me. The fur on its snout wrinkles and I gasp when it shows me its long white incisors. I look at the growling, dog-like creature and can't help but picture it ripping human flesh from a corpse, like the grave-robbing canine I saw earlier in our trip. A low, threatening voice appears in my head saying, "Me and my brothers, we are watching you."

Is it just lizards, wolves, and snakes that scrutinize? Though plenty of desert animals' eyes follow our movements, I can't help feeling like men rather than beasts are stalking us.

What man or men do I fear? Sometimes, fellow travelers talk about being attacked by Indians. Once or twice, I've wondered whether some of the men who walk the trail with us are more dangerous than the ones beyond our ranks. Mostly, fear of the outlaws ahead captures the imagination of our flock. I can't help being swept away by the current, and I constantly scan the horizon in search of unexpected movement.

Then, I wonder whether it is spirits instead that should concern us and remind myself that I don't believe in ghouls. Maybe I'm beginning to believe, more than I'd like to admit. I shut my eyes and quiver as I experience the sensation of ants crawling up my spine.

At the end of the day, I'm relieved to reach the Bear River again. The throbbing scar on my leg reminds me of the silvertip at Little Muddy River. I hope we don't encounter any more of its kind ahead.

Thursday, July 18

Another day of travel brings us to a lovely estuary that flows from a wide canyon. Arikta tells us the waterway is known as Clover Creek.

As we settle into camp, Christopher departs to visit Alvah and Lucky. Andrew works on *The Times*. Stillman helps Dahlia Jane with Gloria's little halter and watches as Dahlia Jane parades the hen around The Hub. My eyes follow Rose, knowing better than to ask her what she's doing. Every time I ask such a question, she snaps at me.

I can't imagine what she'll do with the objects she has gathered. I watch as she grinds charcoal using a mortar and pestle. She runs her fingers through the black dust, and then grinds it even finer. I cringe as I watch her get an egg from the keg of oats. I'd like to stop her and ask her to leave the egg be, scarce as they are. She breaks the shell and separates the yolk from the whites through her fingers. Long strands of gooey egg whites ooze to the dusty ground, wasted. The yellow glob sits in the palm of her hand, and she adds a small amount to the charcoal powder, dropping the rest of the yolk into the campfire. I know I must be frowning at the sight of wasted food. Finally, Rose adds bacon fat to the mixture and stirs it endlessly. What can one make with charcoal dust, egg yolks, and bacon fat? I can't think of a recipe that calls for such a combination.

As if watching her work isn't bad enough, I'm horrified by what I see next. My head begins to pound, and I rub my temples. I hear Larkin's words in my head, telling me that Rose will get through whatever bothers her. If she didn't look wild before, after she applies the dark mixture to her eyelids, she looks like a specter. What has come over her?

I can't restrain myself any longer. I warn myself that I must prepare to hear sharp words, but I can't help it. I walk toward Rose, and say, "What are you doing, honey?"

My child looks up at me and growls. She doesn't even speak. It's the first time I've tried to talk to her in such a moment, and it's the first time she's acknowledged my presence from such a state. I'm scared, and wish she wouldn't behave like this in camp. I don't care what people think of us, but maybe the other children do. As judgmental as our fellow travelers can be, I'm afraid that someone will demand Rose be chained like a wild dog, supposedly for her own protection.

Then, Rose carefully places the black paint in a small jar and stows it in the wagon. It would seem that she intends to use it again in the future. Should I intervene? I rub my forehead arguing back and forth, as mother and father, in my head. Then, Rose walks away without a word to anyone. I want to confront her and tell her that it is rude to walk away and not tell anyone where she's going or when she plans to return. I know she's not going to visit a friend in another wagon. Except for Garland Knox, I don't think she speaks to anybody else, and she barely talks to Garland.

I know I shouldn't let her go. I like Dembi Koofai. If any mother on the wagon train would be inclined to let their daughter marry an Indian, it would be me. She's so young. I try to convince myself that she's older than I think. She has a birthday coming soon. I know that Indian girls marry young. What if Dembi Koofai and Rose asked me to consent to their union? What would I do? What would I say? I know the danger that can come from trying to keep young lovers apart.

Indecision grips me. I'm about to follow, yet my feet feel too heavy to lift from the ground. One second, I decide to run after Rose, and the next second I decide to let nature take its course. The last thing I need this afternoon is a visit from The Committee.

Instead of leading, Captain Meadows follows. Dottie Crouse approaches me, clucking like Gloria at the end of Dahlia Jane's leash. I picture Mrs. Crouse with a beak gripping a stringy worm and squelch the urge to laugh. Dottie sounds like she might lay an egg herself. "I just passed your daughter. She ignored me when I spoke to her. Everyone is talking about the Indian jewelry she wears." Dottie points to her own eyes and says, "Now she wears warpaint. Every day she looks more like an Indian. It just isn't right. She's not a little girl anymore, you know. She shouldn't be walking around alone at her age."

I try to explain Larkin's philosophy on parenting, which is rather unlike that of most men. The Committee doesn't seem to agree much with Larkin's point of view. The best I can offer The Committee is that I will think about their advice and consider their recommendations. Finally, that seems to satisfy them, and I'm relieved when I see Dottie's caboose depart from my campsite.

With a sigh and a heavy heart, I set out to find Rose. I fail to find her, but when I return to camp, she's sitting beside the campfire talking with Andrew as if today were any other day. Her fingers busily twist artemisia into long strands of pungent cordage. Considering the length of the coils at her feet, I must have been gone longer than I thought.

It's not fair to put Andrew in such a position, but I might ask him what he knows about Rose and what she's going through. Sometimes children will tell each other things that they will not share with their parents, but it's late and I'm tired. A conversation with Andrew will have to keep until tomorrow.

FRIDAY, JULY 19

AT SUPPER, WE ENJOY the view of Bald Mountain, to our east. When I turn to glance at Rose, I look into the eyes of the wolf on her choker. A fleeting thought occurs to me. Perhaps I'm as crazy as Rose.

I rub my eyes and look again. I say, "Rose, honey, did you paint the wolf eyes on your necklace?"

Rose utters a guttural sigh. "No. If you must know, Bacon Bump painted them for me." She blinks heavily, showing off her dark eyelids.

I gulp. I don't want to mention my fear of wolves. I try to tear my eyes away, but I can't help staring at them. The color is a perfect match to the eyes of the wolf I saw beneath the sagebrush on Big Hill.

After supper, Rose wanders away. I'm seated close to Andrew, and I speak quietly to him. "Andrew, do you know where Rose goes when she walks off by herself?"

Andrew looks at me like he is surprised by my question. He says, "No, why? She don't pay attention to us most of the time, and we don't pay attention to her neither."

I say, "Oh, I see." After a quiet moment, I add, "I think she has a beau. That's all."

Andrew makes a face. I guess he thinks the idea of someone being sweet on Rose is an unpleasant thought. "Really? Who?"

"I'm not sure. I think I know, but I don't want to say, in case I'm wrong."

Andrew says, "Oh. I'll think about it."

I wonder what he means by, "I'll think about it." I would have expected him to say that he might follow her or perhaps ask around. What good would it do to think about it?

I shrug, pat Andrew on the shoulder, and step over to the master's camp. I notice that Dembi Koofai isn't present and mention it to Agapito.

He says, "We are in Shoshone country. Dembi Koofai is our lead scout in these parts. He spends most of his time in the saddle, on the trail."

I rub my chin and repeat back, "In the saddle, on the trail, eh?" I inhale deeply and exhale slowly.

"Is something troubling you, *estimada*?"

"Many things trouble me, I'm afraid. I suppose you've noticed that Rose wears an Indian choker, a hairdrop, and paints her eyelids black."

"And that worries you, yes?"

"Goodness gracious, I should say so. She's my baby, and yet she's almost a woman also. I'm afraid that she has a beau, and what's worse, she never confides in me. It takes all the patience I can muster not to get angry with her. She treats me like offal, and I let her."

"So you are not upset that she behaves like an Indian. You are not angry that a young man might be sweet on her. It makes you mad that she does not talk to you, yes?"

My cheeks blow wide and I exhale quickly. "Yes, I guess so. Why doesn't she trust me? Why won't she confide in me?"

"Maybe she does not think that you will understand."

"Understand what?"

Agapito's cheeks twist in a strange way. It looks like he's trying to find words to explain what he's thinking. Finally, he says, "Remember when you met Sees Through Clouds at the Birthing Stone?"

"Yes. And Dembi Koofai was there too."

"It sounds like Rose made a spiritual connection there."

"With Dembi Koofai?"

Agapito looks at me like I've lost my mind. "Dembi Koofai? Why Dembi Koofai? No. Sees Through Clouds is the shaman, not Dembi Koofai."

I look down into my lap. Agapito has never talked to me like this before. He sounds impatient, almost irritated.

He says, "I am sorry, *estimada*. Maybe you are too close to the problem to see it clearly, yes? I think Rose wants to be a shaman like Sees Through Clouds. Like Snarling Wolf back in the Brulé camp, remember?"

I shiver at the mention of the Sioux medicine man and remind myself that I should refer to them as Lakota. I say, "I have tried to forget Snarling Wolf."

I take a deep breath and say, "I don't know how Rose can be a shaman. Is it possible for a woman? Is it possible for a white girl?"

"Why not? If it is her dream, should we not help her? If it is her destiny, how could we stop her?"

"Good Heavens, I've never thought about such a possibility. Is a shaman like an Indian priest or priestess?"

"I do not know enough about it. Let me see what I can find out."

"Would Rose have to live with Indians if she were a shaman?"

"I do not know that either, *estimada*."

After I thank him and stand to go, Agapito says, "Sometimes children are a mystery."

It looks like he is speaking from experience. I say, "Sarita?" He shakes his head. "Arikta?" He shakes his head again.

"Dembi Koofai. Sometimes he feels like my child. He is mysterious, no? I try to understand. Maybe someday I will."

After parting with Agapito, I decide to take a walk in the direction Rose went. I'm mesmerized by Bald Mountain, standing tall to the east, and follow my feet toward the towering peak. I hate that Rose feels the need to sneak around in the wilderness to realize her dreams. When I reach the entrance to a deep canyon, I decide that I've gone far enough. I worry that a starving grizzly will get my daughter, and then I hear low voices nearby.

When I follow the sound of people talking, I recognize Rose's voice. The other voice belongs to a man. I peek around a small tree and see Rose sitting on an Indian's lap. His arms encircle her. I don't know what sound comes from me, but they look up at me like I've been caught doing something I shouldn't have done.

I don't think I screamed. I know I gulped and probably gasped. I find my voice and say, "Good Heavens." I may as well have uttered the most ungodly curse words I've ever heard. "Is that you, Mr. Snarling Wolf?"

The Brulé medicine man stands Rose on the ground before him and climbs to his feet in a fluid motion. He reminds me that he said he would follow, that he would wait until Rose became a woman, and that he wouldn't marry her until she fell in love with him. My heart thunders in my chest. I glance at Rose and the eerie eyes of the wolf at her throat glare at me.

All I can think to say is, "I thought that you would forget all about that. I had no idea that you were following the wagon train."

"I do not follow every day. Sometimes yes. Sometimes no."

"How does Rose know when you are here?"

"Sometimes she just knows. Other times, I signal." Snarling Wolf removes a small mirror from a parfleche, and I wonder what else the man carries in that small leather bag.

Rose scowls at me, and I wish I hadn't followed her. Fear consumes me, and my voice cracks when I speak. "Please make sure Rose gets back to camp safely before dark."

He says, "It shall be so."

As I turn away from Snarling Wolf and Rose, hot tears well behind my eyelids. I tell myself that the Brulé medicine man is nice. He loves my daughter, and maybe she loves him. He's a good-looking man, and he seems kind, even if he does seem a little odd. Earlier in the day I wished that Dembi Koofai was younger. Now I wish that Snarling Wolf was as young as Dembi Koofai instead of being ten years older. Why, of all things does he have to worship wolves?

Starting tomorrow, I'll do everything I can think of to find a way to love the man as a future son-in-law. As I make my way back to the wagon, all I can think of is that I wish he would just vanish. Ignoring him after we left Fort Laramie didn't do me any good. I will not make that mistake again.

SATURDAY, JULY 20

LAST NIGHT, WHEN ROSE returned to camp, she climbed into the wagon, closed her eyes, and went to sleep immediately without a word to anyone. Usually, I'm disturbed by the lack of conversation between us, but last night it was a relief. I haven't the foggiest idea what I would have said to her anyway.

This morning, while we prepared for a new day on the trail, all I could think of was the mature shaman's arms wrapped around my daughter's slim body. He's more than twice her age. I stepped through the early-morning darkness into the master's camp and dragged Agapito behind to the opposite side of the wagon and whispered urgently. I would rather the scouts did not witness this, but it could not be helped.

Agapito said, "I understand how you feel. It is common for Indian women to marry young and men to wait until they are older." Though his words are not comforting, I feel better having had the chance to confide in someone. After a quick embrace, I returned to camp and prepared for the day's journey. Yesterday, I promised myself that I would learn to love Snarling Wolf like a son-in-law. First, I must figure out how. If only I could have a breakthrough with Rose.

Now, as we trod along like nothing happened last night, I try to think of a way to introduce the subject that will not make Rose lash out at me. Despite those who would suggest taking a strap to Rose and running off the Indian who follows us, I am sure that would be the wrong thing to do where Rose is concerned. She's a hard one to understand. If this man can help her find her way, and bring her happiness, how can I stand in his way?

After an easy day of travel, we cross a nice creek and circle the wagons. Yesterday, I got all flustered over Rose's problem. Today, I finally decide to leave the matter to fate and baked goods. When camp chores are tended, I stir a batch of scones and add a few drops of the peppermint extract I purchased from Mr. Ray in Independence. I set the Dutch oven beside the fire next to the coffee pot as Agapito appears beside my fire.

Agapito hands me a large chunk of meat. "Here is a gift for you, *estimada*. Our scouts have had a good day hunting, yes?"

He sniffs the air above the Dutch oven and lifts an eyebrow. "I do not smell lemons."

I smile at Agapito and say, "No, not today." I thank him for the meat, and when he's gone, I set a big pot of water over the fire to make stew.

When the scones are finished cooking, I take half, place them in a small basket, and give them to Rose. "These are for you and Snarling Wolf, honey."

Rose looks at me questioningly. It seems as if it was the last thing she expected me to do or say. I can't remember the last time she uttered the words, "Thank you, Mama," but they sure sound sweet today. I watch her sneak away along the creek to the east and sigh. When I was her age,

I yearned for the love of a boy my own age, but nothing good ever came from loving Noah.

When the water boils, I trip when I reach to add diced antelope meat to the pot, upsetting the vessel's balance, and bubbling water soaks my bare foot and shin before I can jump away from the blistering liquid.

I scream so loudly, a crowd gathers. Cobb helps me take a seat. Charlotte runs from two wagons away, and quickly assesses the situation. She shouts, "Take her to the creek and get her foot into the water. I'll get Hollis."

With my leg in the water, I watch as Hollis carries a blanket, rags, and a cushion. When he reaches the creek, he spreads the blanket on the ground and places the cushion on top of it. I lift my leg from the water for his inspection. He says, "That's a bad burn, Dorcas. You're not going to be able to wear shoes for a while. It's going to hurt for a few days. It's going to hurt *a lot*."

Charlotte and Hollis set me on the blanket and prop my leg on the cushion. Then Hollis soaks rags in the creek and covers my foot with them. "You will have to spend most of the day tomorrow just as you are now."

Charlotte says to her husband. "Do you think she could wear a pair of the moccasins I made to give to the Indians?" Her husband approves, and Charlotte retrieves a nice pair of buttery-soft, leather moccasins. She advises, "Don't put them on until tomorrow night, dear."

Finally, I'm left alone on the blanket beside the pleasant creek. I get to thinking about the past couple of days. I suppose Snarling Wolf's presence accounts for the strange feeling I had of being watched.

It occurs to me that I should feel more comfortable now that I know about him, but something still makes me feel uneasy, and it isn't the discomfort of my burn wound or scar where the bear raked my thigh with his claw.

I sit forward and see a rattlesnake slithering toward me. It has the same look in its eyes as the golden snake that had a mouth full of lizard on Big Hill a couple of days ago. I jump to my feet and run, hobbling back to camp, screaming, "Snake. Rattlesnake."

My family settles me into the wagon and props my injured foot on a pillow. Stillman retrieves the moccasins Charlotte gave me from the creek side and returns the borrowed blanket and cushion.

It's not dark yet, but I'm glad to have retired early. The snake has probably disappeared into a hole beside the river. I imagine Rose and Snarling Wolf nibbling peppermint scones in a canyon above camp. Even through the canvas cover, I can't shake the feeling of being watched. Still, something else pursues *us*. Or is it *me* that the menacing eyes seek?

SUNDAY, JULY 21

IF IT WEREN'T FOR the golden rattlesnake, I'd love nothing better than to lie on a blanket beside the creek. Instead, Stillman builds me a throne of boxes, cushions, and blankets beside the wagon. I feel pampered. I'd rather be busy than to laze around watching people come and go, but today I have no choice but to follow doctor's orders. My family will not permit me to do otherwise.

During breakfast, I notice a long white tooth hanging from a rawhide cord around Rose's neck. When I mention it, Rose's fingers flip the fang. Whereas the choker grips her neck, the ivory incisor dangles at the middle of her chest. She confirms that it is a gift from Snarling Wolf and that it comes from a slain grizzly bear. The mention of a lumbering silvertip makes the scar on my thigh throb, though I had been feeling less and less of that pain lately.

Stillman leads the children to Reverend Meadows' creek side Sunday services. I much prefer worshiping God outdoors over praying inside, but I'm not disappointed to be left behind when they go. It is nice to be alone with my thoughts now and then. I'm still trying to talk myself into fully accepting Snarling Wolf, and I find the conversations I have with myself helpful to the cause. When the children return, they tell me that Reverend Meadows asked everyone to pray for me.

Sometimes, doing nothing seems more tiring than keeping busy. Observing the rolling village from my makeshift throne is entertaining for a while, but eventually I grow tired of watching. My eyelids feel heavy. I close my eyes and drift off to sleep. Napping is rarely pleasant on hot, summer afternoons. Even as I surrender to sleep, I'm sweaty just sitting still, and the heat follows me into the world of dreams. One nightmare follows another.

My body hangs in a giant fishing net tied to a rope dangled over an enormous black cauldron. Rose says, "Remember the Donner Party, Mama? We're desperate and we're starving, so we're going to have to eat you." She cackles like a witch and pours a sack of sage into the pot. Snarling Wolf stands behind her, baring his teeth and wrinkling his nose. As Rose lowers me into the seasoned water, my children chant, "Just like Donner, Mama's a goner."

When I awaken from the horrible dream, I see Charlotte. She smiles and dabs my sweaty face with a wet cloth. The doctor's wife says, "That must have been *some* dream. Do you know that you talk in your sleep? I'd hate to have to say the words you were muttering out loud."

"Good heavens, Charlotte. It was awful. My children were going to eat me."

"I know, dear. It was just a nightmare. Try to think of something else. I'll check on you again in a couple of hours." She hands me a full canteen, tells me to drink as much water as I can, and then she's gone.

I watch the heat waves bend the air and swat flies as they land on my skin. After a while, I fall asleep again.

I'm on my back at the bottom of a deep, rectangular-shaped hole. I can see exposed roots at the edges of shovel-cut soil. At the rim of the pit, a pack of growling wolves gaze at me like I'm their next meal. Their slobber rains down on me as slimy serpents writhe upon my naked body. The breeding den of vipers don't seem to care about my presence, except for one, a ten-foot long, gold-colored rattlesnake with a man's face. It's the face of the Frenchman that seduced my hometown. Bartholomieux gives me a lascivious wink, opens his mouth, and wags his serpentine tongue suggestively at me. I awaken, screaming in a feverish sweat.

Instead of wolves looking down at my face, I see Hollis and Charlotte. I look furiously from one set of eyes into another. Charlotte says, "Don't worry dear. Hollis says we should take you back to the river." Charlotte looks into her husband's eyes and then back at me. "He says severe burns can make you feverish and having the auge a month ago might make it worse. We need to cool you down."

"What about the snake?"

"After you burned yourself, did the snake bite you, dear? Is that what's wrong?"

"I don't know. I thought I got away from it. I don't remember feeling like it got me. But the snake lives by the river."

Charlotte frowns. I know she's frightened of them. I remember when she ran screaming from her wagon and jumped into my arms. How long ago was that now? It seems like years. Charlotte says, "Hollis will have to stand guard. I'm not going anywhere near that snake infested crick."

Hollis says, "We mustn't dawdle, darling." The doctor and his wife help me from the wagon, and then Stillman escorts me to the pleasant creek. Hollis follows, and I can hear Charlotte hemming and hawing in the distance as we make our way slowly toward the water.

When my body has cooled, the men help me back to the wagon throne, and Charlotte has a change of clothes ready for me. Instead of letting me wear a pair of Larkin's trousers, she convinces me to wear my pink dress without them.

Late afternoon brings a merciful breeze which cools the skin on my exposed feet, ankle, and shins. I stare at my blistered, elevated foot and wish that I had a long feather to touch it with. I can't help feeling like ants are crawling between my toes. I can feel their tiny feet marching across my skin, even though I can plainly see there aren't any bugs on my feet. It doesn't stop me from sitting up and brushing the invisible insects away. I can't help wondering if I'm starting to go mad, just like Rose. Are these the sort of dark thoughts and frightening feelings that go through her mind sometimes?

As night descends upon us, I pray for sleep devoid of dreams.

Thank you for reading *Stay with the Wagons*. The adventure continues in book number four, with *Snarling Wolf*.

Dive back into the gripping, frontier chaos. The famed Snake River marks the point the wagon master claims that all the greenhorns turn loco. After twelve hundred grueling miles and four relentless months on the trail, the expedition teeters on the brink. Frayed nerves, exhausted patience, and the specter of doom cast a dark cloud over the travelers. Sink your teeth into this tale of survival, madness, and the unyielding spirit of those who brave the treacherous migration. Start reading *Snarling Wolf* today.

I hope to become one of your favorite new authors. Sign up for my email list at: https://www.itsoag.com/contact so you can stay up-to-date on upcoming releases, special offers, and exclusive giveaways. As a thank you, I'll send you a special Ghosts Along the Oregon Trail word search puzzle.

JUMP BACK IN

Don't let the dust settle on your wagon!

Scan the QR code and leap to David Fitz-Gerald's website where you can find the links to the next installment in Ghosts Along the Oregon Trail.

About the Author

David Fitz-Gerald writes westerns and historical fiction. He is the author of twelve books, including the brand-new series, Ghosts Along the Oregon Trail set in 1850. He's a multiple Laramie Award, first place, best in category winner; a Blue Ribbon Chanticleerian; a member of Western Writers of America; and a member of the Historical Novel Society.

Alpine landscapes and flashy horses always catch Dave's eye and turn his head. He is also an Adirondack 46-er, which means that he has hiked to the summit of the range's highest peaks. As a mountaineer, he's happiest at an elevation of over four thousand feet above sea level.

Dave is a lifelong fan of western fiction, landscapes, movies, and music. It should be no surprise that Dave delights in placing memorable characters on treacherous trails, mountain tops, and on the backs of wild horses.

Don't miss Book 4 in the Ghosts Along the Oregon Trail series. Snarling Wolf!

A Tip of the Hat

This series is affectionately dedicated to the countless authors whose words have preserved the legend of the Oregon Trail, the diligent historians who have meticulously chronicled its history, and the brave emigrants who embarked on a perilous journey in pursuit of lofty dreams. Additionally, this series pays tribute to the indigenous peoples whose ancestors lived, loved, and died in these lands since ancient times. The rugged peaks and fruited plains, simultaneously abundant and inhospitable, bore witness to their stories. May their tales always echo through the canyons of history, preserving the spirit and honoring the legacy of those who walked the path before planes, trains, and automobiles.

Thank you to the collaborators that helped me bring Ghosts Along the Oregon Trail to life: editors Kolton Fitz-Gerald and Lindsay Fitzgerald; singer songwriter Kyle Hughes; White Rabbit Arts at the Historical Fiction Company; and the coaches at Author Ad School.

Deep gratitude to my Facebook group, Adirondack Spirit Guides. I appreciate the guidance, support, and early reader feedback. A special nod to Gail Cook, who was the first to make it through the series. Thank you: Cha Abangan, Danielle Apple, Susan Barker, Deva Beeks, Elizabeth Bell, Paul

Bennett, Cecil Betit, Kathleen Bianchi, Bill Buwalda, Wendy Cadieux, Janette Carraway Reynolds, Kate Clifford Eminhizer, Meg Collins, Gail Cook, Tracy Dahl Urschler, Darlene Deans, Keegan Farr, Jeffrey Fitz-Gerald, Patti Fitz-Gerald, D.A. Galloway, Linda Garnett, Janette Gillot, Pam Hough Rogers, Shelbie Howard, Lisa Hunt, TJ London, Jacqueline Marie, Dee Marley, Sandy Miller, Maggie Muir, Steve Murray, Sheila Myers, Anita Ogden, Mary Jane O'Neill, Cody Marie Phoenix, Seth Rain, Dave Reed, Conchita Selvo, Lori Lee Sills, Debra Smith, Chelsie Stanford, Mattie Terrell, Pat Wahler, Quinta Wilkinson, Michelle Willms, and Cindy Yarber Turner.

This project also pays homage to a genre that I've loved as long as I can remember. The old west in fiction, history books, landscape paintings, movies, television and songs inspired this project. If you think a character name is similar to an iconic western hero, you're not mistaken. Some of the characters' names were pulled from the roots of my family tree. For example, a woman named Dorcas is my 6th great-grandaunt. Many monikers are plucked from film credits. The unusual character, Fritz Franzwa is named to honor the work of a dedicated historian who researched, documented, and published *The Oregon Trail Revisited* and *Maps of the Oregon Trail*, which helped me cast my fictional emigrants on credible trail.

During my research for this project, I had the opportunity to visit many of the Oregon Trail's landmarks. It could take a lifetime to visit them all, but I'm well on my way. I've had the pleasure of crisscrossing the historic trail on the scenic byways in Wyoming and Nebraska, and I recall a sweltering day during a record-breaking heatwave in the 1980s. My brother, Jeff, and I visited the mostly abandoned town of Jeffrey City, Wyoming, which boasted a population of three. It's situated near the Oregon Trail and the Sweetwater River. We purchased soft drinks, but by the time we made it back to the truck, the red cans had already gone warm. It was *that* hot. The truck wasn't air conditioned, and I remember sympathizing with the pioneers, trudging along beside a chain of wagons. More recently, I had the pleasure of visiting the National Frontier Trails Museum in Independence, Missouri; the Fort Bridger State Historic Site; and the White Mountain Petroglyphs. It's off the trail, but I just had to send my characters there.

I'm *most* grateful to *you* for stepping away from the present, into the distant past with me. Thank you. I'd love to hear from you. If you get a chance to drop me an email at dave@itsoag.com, I'd love to know: if you were alive in 1850, would you have chosen to follow the Oregon Trail?

Made in the USA
Las Vegas, NV
03 January 2025

15723321R00134